# Power Play in Washington

## Roy MacGregor

An M&S Paperback Original from
McClelland & Stewart Ltd.
*The Canadian Publishers*

For Will Greenblatt and Jonathan Malen, the television
Screech Owls who suggested this story.

The author is grateful to Doug Gibson, who thought up this
series, and to Alex Schultz, who pulls it off.

**National Library of Canada Cataloguing in Publication Data**

MacGregor, Roy, 1948–
    Power play in Washington

(The Screech Owls series; 16)
ISBN 0-7710-5645-1

I. Title. II. Series: MacGregor, Roy, 1948–
Screech Owls series.

PS8575.G84P69 2001    jC813'.54    C2001-901261-6
PZ7.M33PO 2001

We acknowledge the financial support of the Government of
Canada through the Book Publishing Industry Development
Program for our publishing activities.

Cover illustration by Gregory C. Banning
Typeset in Bembo by M&S, Toronto

Printed and bound in Canada

McClelland & Stewart Ltd.
*The Canadian Publishers*
481 University Ave.
Toronto, Ontario
M5G 2E9
www.mcclelland.com

2 3 4 5    05 04 03 02

# 1

BLLLAAAMMM!!!!!!

Travis felt as if the explosion had gone off in his chest. He felt it in his lungs, in his stomach, in the three fillings of his teeth. He felt it right through his hands clapped tightly over his ears since the soldiers with machine guns – *Soldiers! Machine Guns! At a peewee hockey tournament?* – had told the Owls to lie flat on the pavement.

He could see it with his eyes closed. A sudden explosion of red – *his own blood?* – as the pavement seemed to jump.

One thundering explosion, then quiet, and then the sound of clutter falling. Something metal in the distance. Something plastic to his right.

*Something soft on the back of his neck!*

He opened his eyes, the daylight blinding, the air filled with dust from the explosion.

Travis took a hand off one ear and reached back to pull the object off his neck. He was stunned and repulsed by what he saw.

*A filthy pair of old boxer shorts!*

NISH'S!

**WHERE TO BEGIN?**

The Screech Owls had left Tamarack the day before to drive down to Washington, D.C., for the International Goodwill Peewee Championship. They were one of three Canadian teams invited to this spring tournament, and one of several teams from outside the United States.

They had been working for weeks for this moment. They'd held bottle drives and bingos. They'd auctioned off a pair of tickets for a game between the Toronto Maple Leafs and the Detroit Red Wings.

Mr. Dillinger and coach Muck Munro had taken turns driving on the way down. Everyone was in a great mood, though the Owls got fed up with Nish's non-stop tapping on the window – *tap-tap . . . tap-tap-tap . . . tap-tap* – and forced him to sit on an inside seat where he couldn't bug them any longer. It was always something with Nish. A new yell, a new way of talking – and now a stupid rhythm he couldn't get out of his head and soon his teammates couldn't get out of theirs.

Mr. Dillinger had called for a "Wedgie Stop" just after the border so they could all stretch their legs and loosen up their underwear. And he'd stopped *twice* for "Stupid Stops" – Nish stocking up on plastic vomit and sponge toffee and huge cannon cracker fireworks that weren't legal at home.

He used the plastic vomit to gross out Simon Milliken and Jenny Staples, and a couple of hours later, after six straight sponge toffees, grossed out drivers passing by on Interstate 70 with his own, real-life vomit while poor Mr. Dillinger stood beside him handing over paper towels – but that's another story altogether.

The Screech Owls had made it to their very first practice at the MCI Center, the huge downtown NHL arena where the Washington Capitals played. The Owls had rarely been so excited to get to a new rink, and it wasn't just because this was the home of the Caps. Right after the Owls, the Washington Wall were scheduled to practise. And everyone knew about the Wall, the team with the most famous peewee hockey player of the moment: Chase Jordan – the twelve-year-old son of the President of the United States.

Everything had seemed fine, at first.

Nish, looking a bit green, had got off the bus first and headed up a back street for a little air. All the other Owls had gone to the back of the old bus to help Mr. Dillinger get the equipment out.

It was a ritual they could do without thinking. Derek Dillinger was up at the rear door, helping his dad and Muck toss down the bags. Wilson and Willie and Andy, three of the bigger Owls, were carting the equipment bags to the side and stacking them with Fahd's help. Travis and Jesse got Sam and Sarah to help with Mr. Dillinger's skate-sharpening machine. Jeremy and Jenny took care of their own goaltending equipment. Simon and Lars and Dmitri carried the sticks over to Gordie and Liz, who stacked them and sorted them out according to players' numbers. Data, working from his wheelchair, ticked off the equipment on a special sheet he and Fahd had designed to keep track of it all.

They were almost finished when a large van sped around the back of the big rink, squealed to a halt, and four men jumped out. They were all big, all in suits, and each had a small earplug in his left ear with a clear plastic wire coiling down inside the back of his shirt collar. They all wore sunglasses, Travis noticed. He also noticed the handgun that flashed briefly in its holster before one of the men caught his flapping jacket and buttoned it quickly.

"*What do you think you're doing?*" the lead man had barked at the Screech Owls.

Mr. Dillinger, sweat pouring down his face, smiled from beneath his big moustache.

"We have the ice booked at three for a practice," he said.

The man ripped a sheet of paper out of his vest pocket and studied it.

"Screech Owls?" the man said. It was more accusation than question.

Mr. Dillinger nodded. "We're from Canada."

The man paid no attention. He snapped the gum he was frantically chewing and flashed his badge at Mr. Dillinger, who had no time to read it.

"Secret Service," the man said. "We have to secure the building."

"President's son?" Mr. Dillinger asked.

The man offered no answer. He turned to where the kids were stacking the equipment bags.

"*Pull those equipment bags over here and line them up!*" he shouted.

"We're on in twenty minutes!" Mr. Dillinger protested. "We have to dress!"

The man paid no attention. He signalled his three colleagues to move into action. Each one grabbed two bags and half-carried, half-dragged them over to a roped-off area at the rear of the parking area. They laid the bags out in a row.

"*Get your bags over there and put them the same way!*" the lead man barked.

Muck, who hadn't said a word so far, signalled the kids to do as the man said. Travis moved his bag over and dropped it beside Sarah's.

"This is ridiculous!" Sarah whispered as they turned back.

"It's like a movie," Travis said.

5

"A *stupid* movie."

"*Okay!*" the lead man shouted when Lars had dropped the last bag in line. "*Now back off against the building. And no sudden movements!*"

Sam rolled her eyes at Travis.

"*Look!*" gasped Sam.

Another van had pulled up. Its doors opened, and this time two soldiers with large dogs on leashes got out.

"Sniffer dogs," said Fahd.

"What for?" said Sam.

"Standard Secret Service procedure," explained Fahd, who always knew such things. "They secure any building first where a member of the First Family's going to be. We better get used to it."

"What a *pain*," groaned Sarah.

The dogs were frisky. One was a German shepherd, the other a black Labrador. They seemed more interested in playing with each other and their handlers, but one sharp hand signal from each handler and the dogs instantly went to work.

The dogs started at opposite ends of the long line of bags. They sniffed up and down, in the side pockets and around each bag, then moved on, with their handlers holding tight to the leashes.

Suddenly, the Labrador's tail stopped moving. The Lab crouched down. The hair on its back rose. It lay down, muzzle pointing towards one of the bags.

The lead man now shouted excitedly into his wrist, "*K-9 Four! K-9 Four!*"

"He's gone off the deep end," Lars giggled.

"It's a wrist radio," Fahd explained. "Code for something."

There were sirens now. And it seemed the temperature had suddenly risen even further.

The Secret Service men were scurrying. One shouted "*Explosives positive!*" into his own wrist radio.

"Whose bag is it?" Dmitri asked.

Travis craned his neck to catch the number stencilled on the side of the bag.

Forty-four.

Nish's bag.

*The firecrackers from the Stupid Stop!*

Travis shouted out to Muck and Mr. Dillinger that it was Nish's bag, and Mr. Dillinger, understanding immediately, had tried to catch the attention of the lead Secret Service man – but there was near panic now, and no one would listen to him.

Within moments the area had been cleared, blocked off, and the Owls had been told to lie flat on the pavement and not to lift their heads.

But even so, they could still see much of what was happening.

An armoured vehicle arrived almost immediately. Soldiers scurried to move away all the equipment bags the dogs had checked, leaving just the one – number 44 – in the centre of the cordoned-off area.

Another vehicle screeched to a halt and its back door opened.

A ramp extended from the doorway, and a shiny metal robot rolled out. Directly behind it walked a heavily armoured soldier fiddling with a control box.

"A bomb robot!" whispered Fahd.

"What for?" asked Wilson.

"They're checking the bag for a bomb!"

"Maybe they should be checking it for poisonous gas!" giggled Sarah.

"*Shut up over there!*" barked the lead Secret Service man. He was still furiously snapping his chewing gum.

The Owls went silent. They watched, helplessly, as the robot whirred over to the bag, seemed to take photographs of it, then backed off.

Soldiers gathered around the man with the control box, studying its screen.

Yet another armoured vehicle arrived. Two soldiers, also heavily armoured, scurried out. One held a huge, bazooka-like gun. Several other vehicles backed away quickly.

The two soldiers took up position, one holding the weapon, the other aiming it.

"*They're going to blow up Nish's bag!*" Sam said, her voice skipping between a scream of terror and one of absolute delight.

## 3

BLLLAAAMMM!!!!!!

It wasn't just Nish's filthy old jockey shorts that rained down upon the cringing Owls.

Sarah got hit with a T-shirt, its armpits yellow and with what seemed like half an old pizza hanging from it. The front said, "Welcome to Lake Placid."

Half-eaten chocolate bars rained down, torn strings of red and green licorice, a broken pen with a girl in a bathing suit on it, smashed X-ray glasses, ripped comic books, torn hockey cards, once-white socks as hard as hockey pucks, smashed water bottles, tools to fix televisions, burst ketchup packs, fungus-covered French fries, old lacrosse balls, grade five, six, and seven workbooks, balls of used shin-pad tape, smashed videotapes and Nintendo games, cracked and empty CD cases, a busted fake Rolex watch, a wizened orange that had turned almost green, burst Coke tins, bent shin pads, torn shoulder pads, ripped Screech Owls home and away jerseys, a thumb from a hockey glove, and a helmet with a plastic visor smashed worse than the windshield of a car that had run into a brick wall.

"MY STUFF!"

The cry came from the far end of the parking lot. Travis didn't even have to lift his head to know who had called out.

Nish was standing at the corner of the rink staring in disbelief at the assembly of army trucks and soldiers and anti-bomb equipment. He was, if anything, looking even greener than when he'd walked off to "get some air." The air was still filled with smoke and fluttering pieces of card – Nish's precious stash of his own hockey cards from Quebec City.

"*What have you done to my equipment!*" Nish wailed.

The lead Secret Service guy was walking fast toward Nish, frantically brushing debris off his suit.

"*Who the hell are you?*" the Secret Service man demanded, his teeth ripping into his gum.

"Wayne . . . Nishikawa," Nish answered. He looked like he was about to throw up again.

"You with this team?"

"Yeah."

"Well, we had to blow up your equipment."

"Why?"

"Dog sniffed explosive. You have explosives in there, son?"

Nish put on his finest choirboy look and shook his head.

"Just my hockey stuff, sir," he said.

"Well," the Secret Service man snapped, turning on his heels. "You'll have to get new stuff now." He walked away, leaving Nish astonished.

The Owls were on their feet, dusting themselves off and picking up pieces of Nish's equipment. Lars held a skate blade high, shaking his head as he stared at it.

"*There's nothing left!*" Nish wailed.

"There's this, Big Boy!" Sam shouted.

She threw something at him. He caught it in the air and held it up.

It was yellowish-white, torn and smouldering, smoke rising from holes that had been peppered through it by the explosion.

A metal cup fell from it and clattered on the pavement.

"They even blew up my jock!" Nish moaned. "I'VE NOTHING LEFT TO WEAR!"

## 4

SAM AND SARAH WERE IN THE DRESSING ROOM, kneeling at opposite ends of Nish's new equipment bag, when Nish stepped out of the washroom, his hair freshly watered down and parted for the practice. Both girls had their heads buried in the open bag, and both, at the moment he appeared, sat back and, eyes closed, made a grand display of drinking in the air from the bag.

"Ahhhhhh," Sam said, inhaling deeply. "Like a garden of flowers!"

"Like a spring shower," Sarah agreed. "We could call it 'Breeze of Nish' and sell it."

"Get outta there!" Nish shouted, blood racing to his face. "Or I'll give you a breeze that'll peel paint off the walls."

"Such a charmer," Sam giggled as she and Sarah backed away and Nish took up his usual seat in the corner farthest from the door.

The bag in front of him was an Owls equipment bag, but the number, 44, was scribbled on in grease pencil rather than stitched. Mr. Dillinger had scrambled to replace Nish's destroyed hockey equipment, and he'd done an amazing job.

Carrying extra skates in the general equipment bag had paid off; there was a pair of size 8s that Andy had outgrown but which fitted Nish almost perfectly. There were extra pads and gloves and a pair of pants that Mr. Dillinger had stitched up. Mr. Dillinger even produced new team socks for Nish and a new sweater. Not his old 44, of course, which had been destroyed in the explosion, but 22. "Some people say you're only half there, anyway," Mr. Dillinger had joked, and even Nish had been forced to laugh.

But he was hardly happy now.

"This isn't me!" Nish had moaned when he was finally suited up.

"*Thank God!*" Sarah and Sam had shouted out at the same time.

"I'm missing my 'A,'" he whined.

"We can fix that," said Mr. Dillinger. He pulled out a roll of tape, cut three strips, and stuck them on to form a quick assistant captain's "A."

"And I'm missing my lucky shorts!" Nish groaned, almost in tears.

"*Lucky us!*" shouted Sam.

"I've worn them since Lake Placid!" he muttered.

"*When?*" Travis asked, eyes widening in disbelief.

"Lake Placid," Nish repeated.

Travis, like every other Owl in the room, did some rapid mental calculations. *Months* had passed since the tournament in Lake Placid. *Hundreds* of games and practices. *Surely he hadn't worn the same pair of boxer shorts in every one of them!*

"You must have washed them?" Fahd asked, equally incredulous.

Nish shook his head. "Only a fool would wash off good luck," he groaned.

"It's a wonder Washington is still standing!" laughed Sarah.

Nish said nothing. He leaned back in his stall, closed his eyes, and stuck out his tongue in the general direction of everyone in the room.

Muck threw one of his "curve balls" into the practice. After they had worked on a new break-out pattern and taken shots at Jenny and Jeremy, Muck had them all toss their sticks over the boards and onto the bench floor while Mr. Dillinger struggled out from the dressing room area with a large, open cardboard box.

"Everyone take one!" ordered Muck. "And *no* reloading!"

Travis looked at Nish, who scowled back. What was Muck up to?

Lars's hand was first into the box. He pulled out a green, clear plastic water gun, water dripping from the plug and trigger. Wilson got a blue one. Sarah got a red one. Hands plunged into the box, each one emerging with a cheap, filled-to-the-brim water gun.

"Have fun," Muck said, and stepped off the ice, hurrying up the corridor towards the Owls' dressing room before anyone could think to take a shot in his direction.

"What're we supposed to do with these?" Nish asked, holding his up like he'd never seen one before.

"*This!*" Sam shouted, squirting him straight in his open mouth.

She took off down the ice, Nish chasing. Bedlam broke out at the bench as Owls began firing at Owls. Screaming and yelling and laughing, they chased each other around the rink, trying to get a shot in.

Andy and Simon went after Travis, but he was too agile a skater for them to nail him with a good blast. He twisted behind the goal. He used the net for a shield. He scooted out and towards the blue-line and then turned back so fast his skates almost lost their edge.

Everywhere, the Owls were twisting and turning and ducking and trying to cut each other off. Travis slipped back behind the net again, jockeying for position as Simon came in from the left.

Travis faked one way, then turned back on Simon, blasting him as he twisted and coiled back along the boards.

Travis realized what Muck had done. They were playing – but they were also practising! They might not have sticks or pucks, but they were still working on hockey skills. Twisting and turning along the boards was not unlike cycling in the corners. Racing for the net was not unlike looking for a scoring chance. Trying to cut off a player who'd just sprayed you and was now racing down the ice was not unlike trying to read the ice to make a check.

It made Travis laugh to think how brilliant Muck could sometimes be. The Owls would be convinced this was nothing but messing around – and yet they were probably learning far more about hockey than they were about water pistols.

Nish, naturally, ran out of water first.

When the others realized this, they turned on him as a team. Nish cowered in the corner with his hands held up helplessly to block the spray of more than a dozen water guns. Finally, the last spurt went down his neck, and Nish rose up in a rage and began blindly chasing the scattering attackers.

They were saved by a shrill whistle from the bench. Muck's whistle. Everyone stopped dead in their tracks and turned to glide towards the bench where Muck was standing, whistle still in his mouth, face red with anger.

Beside Muck was Mr. Dillinger with the box that had held the water pistols, and behind them was the Secret Service leader, earplug still in, teeth still snapping on his chewing gum. He looked stern.

"Put 'em away, kids," Mr. Dillinger said. "Security says you gotta hang 'em up."

"What's wrong?" asked Sam, as she tossed her empty pistol into the box.

"Water pistols," Muck said quietly through clenched teeth, "are apparently a 'security breach' in this rink."

"Just while the tournament's on, Coach," the gum-snapper said. "We have to confiscate them and they'll be returned to you before you head back home."

"*Water* pistols?" said Sarah.

Travis studied Muck. He knew that the quieter Muck spoke the more upset he was bound to be. He also knew that Muck hated to be called "Coach." It was an American thing, he always said. Hockey was a Canadian game, and his name was the same whether he stood behind the bench or out in the parking lot: Muck Munro.

"Any kind of pistol, miss," the man said. "Replicas, facsimiles, toys – whatever. One of my men sees one of these being pointed, and we shoot first and ask questions later, understand?"

Nish didn't. "Like what?" he asked. "'Are you using hot or cold water?'"

"Don't be smart, mister," the man said. "I have authority to suspend any team or player from this tournament we deem to be a security risk – and you've already got one count against you, do you not?"

Nish flushed deep red. He said nothing more.

Mr. Dillinger took the last of the pistols, folded the flaps of the box, and handed it over to the security head, who tossed it to an assistant.

"Three times around," Muck said to the Owls. "Skate it out of you. Let's go now!"

Muck blew his whistle sharply three times. The man with the earplug winced, and Travis grinned to himself. Muck rarely blew his whistle, and never hard. This was just his way of taking a shot at the security head. Good for Muck!

Travis skated with Sarah, the two of them talking about the absurdity of the situation and laughing, again, at how helpless Nish had looked when the team had him down in the corner and was spraying him at will.

"Look over there," Sarah said suddenly, tilting her head towards the opposite side of the ice.

A kid their age – curly red hair, blue eyes – was standing so close to the glass at the visitors' doorway that his breath was fogging it up.

He was in full uniform, holding his helmet in one hand and a stick in the other. He stared at the Owls as they left the ice.

"Earplug's watching him," said Sarah.

Behind the youngster, studying him with fierce concentration, was the Secret Service head, the man who chewed gum like a beaver going through a branch.

Travis giggled. Earplug was a perfect nickname for him.

Beyond Earplug stood another three men, each facing in a different direction, each standing on the balls of his feet as if he might, on a moment's notice, have to tackle someone.

Travis and Sarah stared back.

"Guess who the kid is," Sarah said.

Travis knew – the President's son, the centre for the Washington Wall.

He was so close to the glass it was almost as if he were trying to push through.

Travis understood. All his life, a hockey rink and especially a clean, untouched ice surface, had been his own greatest escape. It must be worth even more, he realized, to the son of the President of the United States.

Sarah took off her glove and waved to the boy.

Unsure, the boy lifted his hand and gave a quick wave back.

Behind him, the Secret Service man snapped his gum and scowled.

## 5

TRAVIS WAS THE FIRST TO WAKE IN THE LITTLE hotel room he was sharing with Nish and Fahd and Lars. Nish was still snoring. He'd managed to turn completely around in the large double bed he was sharing with Fahd, and his toes were resting on the pillow beside Fahd's head. Poor Fahd, thought Travis. What a sight to wake up to!

Sunlight was streaming in the window. There were dust particles dancing in the air – "angels," Travis's grandmother called them – and he watched for a while, wondering how they avoided the pull of gravity that ruled everything else on earth. Perhaps his grandmother was right.

Mr. Dillinger was filled with plans for the day. They would walk around the Capitol building, down the Mall to take in the view from the top of the towering Washington Monument, and on through the park and across the bridge to Arlington Cemetery. Then they'd walk back to the Smithsonian Air and Space Museum to see the *Spirit of St. Louis* and the spacesuit worn by Neil Armstrong, the first man on the moon, before returning to the hotel to rest before the first game of the tournament.

The Owls had drawn team number one in the round robin – Djurgården, from Stockholm, Sweden. Lars, who knew some of the players, had already warned the Owls that they would be in for a tremendous battle. Travis could hardly wait.

They set out in weather so beautiful it seemed impossible that there were still deep snowbanks back home. Here, the cherry trees were in full blossom as they headed out into the park, Muck and Mr. Dillinger leading the way, Sarah helping guide Data's chair. They walked to the huge, open-air Lincoln Memorial, where Muck insisted on reading, out loud, Abraham Lincoln's Gettysburg Address: "Four score and seven years ago . . ."

"I thought this was a hockey tournament," Nish whispered in Travis's ear, "not a history class."

Travis said nothing. He knew how Muck loved his history, and knew, as well, how much Nish hated anything to do with school that wasn't recess, March break, or summer holidays. But there was no point in arguing. Nish had already wandered off, fascinated with the echoes he could produce by tapping a small stone against the marble: *tap-tap . . . tap-tap-tap . . . tap-tap.* Where was security when you actually needed it?

They set out across the bridge over the Potomac River and up into the gently rolling slopes of

Arlington National Cemetery, where they walked quietly about the Tomb of the Unknown Soldier and the graves of President John F. Kennedy and his younger brother, Bobby. Bobby might one day have become president too, if he hadn't been shot like his brother. Muck seemed deeply moved. With his eyes shining, he tried to explain to them what the Kennedys had meant to people like him and Mr. Dillinger.

"Everything seemed possible back then," he said in a quiet voice. "They were so young and so full of life. We all wonder what the world might have become if they had lived. If it hadn't been for John Kennedy, you know, the world wouldn't have reached the moon."

"If it hadn't been for Ol' Nish," Nish whispered in Travis's ear, "the world wouldn't have *seen* the moon."

Nish could never leave well enough alone. Muck was talking about space travel and as usual Nish wanted to talk about himself. Besides, he was exaggerating. Maybe Nish had planned to moon the world in New York City, but he hadn't done it. Fortunately.

"Why were they killed?" Fahd asked.

Muck shrugged. "Presidents are always in danger of being assassinated. We'll see where Abraham Lincoln was killed at Ford's Theatre. It's not far from the rink. And Ronald Reagan was shot right back there, near the Capitol and surrounded by Secret Service. There's no pattern, which is why it's so difficult to defend against. It's usually just some nut."

"What about the President's kids?" Jenny asked.

Muck furrowed his brow. "They have to be protected, too," he said. "You never know what some lunatic might try."

"Is that why there's all that Secret Service stuff around the hockey tournament," Lars asked, "because they're worried about the kid?"

"That's one reason," Muck said.

"There's another?" Data asked.

Muck nodded.

"What?" several of the Owls said at once.

Muck smiled sheepishly. "I'm not really supposed to say . . ."

"You *have* to now," Jesse shouted.

"Well," Muck said, "just don't broadcast it around."

"We won't!" shouted Fahd. "What is it?"

"The championship trophy is going to be presented by the President."

Travis swallowed hard. It felt like he was trying to push a pill the size of a puck down his throat. If the President of the United States was going to be presenting the trophy to the winning team of the championship, then he would be giving it to the captain of the winning team.

And if the Screech Owls won, that would be Travis Lindsay.

## 6

DJURGÅRDEN SKATED OUT IN THE SWEDISH national team colours: beautiful yellow sweaters with the three crowns of Sweden in blue crests across their fronts. They looked intimidating, the sort of team that is so skilled, so fluid, and so organized that they can sometimes defeat the other team before the warm-up is even over.

Travis was particularly nervous. He missed the crossbar on five straight shots in warm-up. He tried to figure out what was wrong but couldn't quite put his finger on it. The first game of a big tournament? It shouldn't be that. All the security?

"This doesn't *feel* right," a voice squeaked in his ear.

He knew at once it was Nish. He was relieved to discover his friend was also uneasy.

But for different reasons.

"I need my old boxer shorts back," Nish whined.

"They're in the garbage. Go pick 'em out," Travis laughed.

"They're ruined. I should sue."

"Sue the government of the United States of America for your boxers?" Travis asked.

"They had no right to destroy them."

"They have the undying gratitude of our whole hockey team," Travis said.

"*Nothing* feels right," Nish continued, not listening to anything Travis was saying. "I've got the wrong shorts on. Wrong equipment. Everything's wrong. I don't even *smell* like me!"

"God bless America!" Travis said, and skated away from his muttering, mumbling pal.

What a difference an ocean made! When the Owls went to Sweden, they were baffled at first by the big Olympic ice surface. Now the Djurgården peewees had the same problem in reverse. To them, the ice was cramped and tight. Less space meant less time, and they were panicking with the puck. Used to being able to work the corners, they now had to fight for them, and the usual long cross-ice passes of European hockey were easy pickings for the Owls – particularly for a player as quick as Dmitri.

Dmitri scored the first two goals. He snared a lazy Swedish pass in the neutral zone, roared in on the opponents' net, faked once, went to his backhand and roofed the puck, sending the water bottle flying. On the second, he finished off a pretty tic-tac-toe play where Travis slipped the puck back to Sarah, moving in late on a rush, and Sarah snapped the puck ahead to Dmitri as he came to a spraying stop at the far goal post.

Dmitri had only to redirect the puck in behind the falling goaltender.

"They'll find themselves," Muck warned at the first break. "Just like you guys had to find yourselves over there."

Muck was right. In the second period, the Swedes adjusted their game. Forwards carried less and shortened their passes. Defencemen used the boards more, pinching in on the Owls whenever they could and causing pucks to jump free. The first Djurgården goal came on a scramble, and then a fluid-skating centre scored a beautiful goal on a solo rush when he managed to slip the puck between Nish's legs and get in alone on Jenny.

"Never would have happened if I'd had my old boxers on," a red-faced Nish muttered when he plunked down on the bench.

"The puck would have *melted*!" laughed Sam, plunking down beside him and giving him a shot in the shoulder.

Both teams scored in the third, Djurgården on a tip, and Lars on a beautiful end-to-end rush with a hard backhander along the ice that just caught the corner.

Muck called a time-out with two minutes to go and hardly said a word. There was really nothing to say. Everyone knew how much a win mattered in a round robin. Travis also knew that Muck wanted his top line out for the final moments, and Sarah was gasping for breath, having just killed off a penalty.

Nothing had gone right for Travis. He had the one assist, but nothing more. The one good shot he'd had slipped off his blade and flopped off to the side of the net. He thought the other team might even be laughing at his weak shot. He needed something. Anything.

Nish and Sam were back. The most powerful five Owls had the ice, and Sarah won the faceoff by sweeping it back to Nish. Nish moved back behind his own net, checking the clock quickly and then measuring the ice for the best side to go up.

He faked a pass to Travis along the left boards and then shot it back off the boards to Sam on the other side.

Nish moved out quickly, "accidentally" brushing by the forechecker to put him off balance and give Sam more time. Sam used it to step around the second forechecker and fire a hard pass up-centre to Sarah, who was curling just before the red line.

Dmitri was already away down the right side. Sarah dumped the puck in as she crossed centre, and Dmitri beat the Djurgården defence to it.

Dmitri danced with the puck out to the open corner. Travis cut for the slot, slapping his stick on the ice.

Dmitri hit him perfectly.

Travis tucked the puck in to himself as he drifted around the last defenceman. He had an open shot – and fired hard. The goaltender jumped, literally leaving the ice, and the puck hit him high in the chest pad and dropped back down in the crease.

Travis was still moving in. He saw the puck there, patiently waiting for him, as the goalie came back down on his skates, scraping hard and falling off to the other side.

Open net!

Travis stabbed at the free puck just as a glove lunged out of nowhere and yanked it to the side and out of harm's way.

Travis could not stop his stab. He hit air, then fell, tearing the net off its moorings as he was hit from behind.

He could see nothing. All he could hear was the referee's whistle, so close it seemed to be screaming. He rolled over, looking back to see what the call was and who had hit him. At least he had drawn a penalty, he figured. Not as good as a goal, but not bad.

But the referee was not pointing at any of the Djurgården players. He was pointing hard towards centre ice.

Travis was momentarily confused. He knew the signal from somewhere. Had he seen it in the rule book? Had he seen it on television?

Suddenly it came to him.

*Penalty shot!*

## 7

"NUMBER SEVEN – WHITE!"

Travis didn't need to hear it again. He knew what the referee's call meant. He'd been closest to the puck when the Djurgården defenceman had put his hand over the puck in the crease. The penalty-shot call was automatic.

"A penalty shot has been awarded to the Screech Owls," the PA system crackled throughout the arena. "The shot will be taken by number seven, Travis Lindsay."

Travis got shakily to his feet. It wasn't because of the hit that he felt wobbly.

He skated slowly to the bench, where Muck was leaning over, a big arm open for Travis to skate into. If only the arm would open up like a cave and swallow me, thought Travis. If only they'd called out number nine for Sarah, or ninety-one for Dmitri, or even forty-four – no, *twenty-two!* – for Nish. *Anybody but me!* But outwardly Travis managed to remain calm. Muck's big arm around his shoulders helped.

So did Muck's voice, so soft and reassuring.

"There's a secret to the penalty shot, you know," Muck said.

"What?" Travis asked, desperate to know.

"Shoot," Muck said, and smiled down at him. "Some guys get so excited they forget to shoot. Just shoot the puck and see what happens."

Travis nodded. He felt like he couldn't talk.

The linesman was placing the puck at centre ice. Only the officials, the Djurgården goaltender, and Travis Lindsay were on the ice.

The referee blew his whistle and swung his arm to indicate it was time.

Travis circled back on his own side of centre. He could hear the crowd cheering. He could hear his teammates thumping their sticks against the boards.

He picked up the puck and felt it wobble at the end of his blade. He almost lost it immediately.

He dug in. He hadn't noticed how much snow was on the ice, but they'd played the entire game and there had been no flood. Now it seemed there was snow everywhere! The ice was chopped up and gouged and the snow seemed to have piled up so deep in front of him he needed a plough to get through.

He felt his legs turn to rubber, his stick to boiled spaghetti. He felt his hands weaken, his shoulders sag. He felt his brain begin to race like a motor at full throttle. He felt his eyes go out of focus, his hips stop moving, his spine collapse, his brain spring apart like the rubber in a sliced golf ball.

He was on a breakaway – a penalty shot in an international tournament – and he was screwing up!

Time had never gone so slow, and at the same moment so fast.

He looked up. The Djurgården goaltender seemed completely at ease. He had come out to cut off the angle, and now was reading Travis perfectly and wiggling his way back toward the net, always with the angle right, giving away nothing.

What do I do? Travis wanted to shout. Deke him?

Blast away?

Fake the shot and try and get the angle?

Go five hole?

Backhand?

Forehand?

He wanted to stop dead in his tracks, turn to the bench and scream, "MUCK! WHAT DO I DOOOOO?"

But there was no time. The referee was skating alongside him now, watching. The little Swedish goaltender was wiggling back into his crease and still had given Travis nothing to shoot at.

*There's too much snow!*

*The ice is too bad!*

*I need to circle back and come in again!*

It was too late. He was in too close. He decided, at the last moment, to go backhand, and flicked the puck over from his forehand.

*The puck slid away from him!*

Travis jabbed at it. He hit the puck badly with the blade of his stick. It skipped towards the corner. He lunged, swinging madly at the puck and catching it with the heel of his stick.

The puck shot towards the net, narrowly missing the post – but on the wrong side!

The whistle blew, the Djurgården bench erupted – Travis started to turn away from the net, lost his edge, and fell, sliding into the boards.

He could hear people in the crowd laughing.

He got up, knocked the snow off – *See*, he wanted to yell, *look at the snow!* – and headed back to a bench where no one was cheering, where hardly anyone was even looking at him.

He had failed the Owls.

Sarah gave him a sympathetic smile, but it wasn't what Travis needed. He needed a second chance.

Muck had his big fists jammed deep in the pockets of his old windbreaker. He was half smiling, half shaking his head.

"Shoot next time," Muck said in his very quiet voice.

Travis nodded. Inside, he was bawling.

# 8

TRAVIS HAD NO IDEA HOW LONG HE'D BEEN standing at the urinal. He'd come off the ice with the rest of the Owls – the silence crushing as they slouched their way back to the dressing room – and he'd set his stick against the wall, lopped off his helmet, dropped his gloves, and hurried off to the little washroom. He didn't need to go. He'd just wanted to get away.

He stood there, waiting, all through the low rumble of Muck's short post-game speech. He knew what Muck would be saying: *Good effort, good work, lucky to come out of it with a tie, we'll just have to be a little sharper next game . . .* He could hear Mr. Dillinger putting away the skate sharpener and bundling up the sticks, lightly whistling as he worked, the way he always did when there was a bit of tension in the dressing room.

Travis felt terrible. He felt he'd failed the team. He felt he should rip the "C" off his sweater and hand it back. A captain was supposed to lead by example, or so Muck always said, and what an example Travis had set:

Blow the penalty shot.

Give up the win when it is yours for the taking.

Choke under pressure.

Travis stood there until he knew he could put it off no longer. He buckled up and headed back in to face the jury.

As he came through the door, he pretended to be absorbed in lacing up his hockey pants. The Owls were all busy shedding their gear. There was the familiar smell of *hockey* in the air, a steely, damp, and sweaty smell found nowhere else on earth but a dressing room in the minutes following a hard-fought game.

Fahd looked up first, one of his ridiculous questions rising.

"Where were *you*?" Fahd asked accusingly.

"Going to the bathroom," Travis said, trying to sound matter-of-fact.

Nish looked up, grinning like a red tomato.

"Did you miss *that*, too?" Nish giggled.

The dressing room exploded with laughter.

"Nish is a goof," Fahd said to Travis as they backed out through the door with their equipment.

"You're just realizing that?" Travis said. His voice made him sound angrier than he was. He wasn't upset with Nish — at least, not as much as he was with himself.

The bus was parked behind the MCI Center, and the fastest way out was through the Zamboni chute. They pushed through a second door, neither one saying a word, and began to walk across the drainage grating alongside the Zamboni.

"DON'T MOVE!"

Travis and Fahd froze in their tracks. It was like being in a movie. Someone they couldn't see had barked a command. *What was next? Gunfire?*

A shadow emerged from the far side of the Zamboni.

Earplug!

He was snapping his gum and had one hand just inside his jacket as if prepared to pull out his .38 snubnose Smith & Wesson and blow the two Screech Owls away.

"What're you two doing here?" Earplug snapped.

"We just played a game," said Fahd. "We're leaving."

"Door's that way, smart fellow!" Earplug barked, nodding in the opposite direction.

"Our bus's out back," said Fahd.

Earplug seemed to think about that a moment. There was no sound at all in the room but the grind of his teeth and the periodic little *snap-snap-snap* as he flicked his tongue through the gum.

Like a snake! Travis thought. A gum-chewing snake!

Finally, it seemed to register on Earplug. The bus *could* be out back. The shortest route between dressing room and back parking lot was indeed through the Zamboni chute and out the back door.

He nodded to himself and stepped back for them to pass. He waved them along with his one free hand, as if directing traffic.

Travis could hardly believe how jumpy Earplug was. He seemed almost out of control – one hand waving two peewee hockey players through to the parking lot, the other hand on his concealed weapon as if, any second now, he'd be forced to blow them away.

"Th–thanks," said Fahd.

The two Owls squeezed by. The Zamboni had been opened up so Earplug and his security force could check the insides. Travis could see the blades that sent the shaved ice up into the holding tank and the hydraulic pistons that dumped the snow out. What did he think? Travis wondered. That one of the Zamboni drivers might sneak out with the machine during play, slip up behind the President's son during a faceoff, gobble him up, and then race out the back doors to hold him for ransom? Travis giggled to himself at the thought of the chase: police cars, fire engines, helicopters all chasing the chugging Zamboni down Pennsylvania Avenue.

Ludicrous, he thought.

But still, he had to give Earplug credit. He was thorough.

## 9

FAHD TURNED THE TELEVISION ON. HE WANTED to play the hotel's in-house Nintendo, but Travis caught him before he switched it over.

"There's the White House!" Travis almost shouted.

"So?" Fahd said. "It's CNN. It's always got the stupid news on."

"Yeah, but that's live – and it's just around the corner."

Fahd paused. "Yeah, weird."

They watched for a few moments. It was a report of a big summit on the Middle East Peace Accord, and there were shots of limousines arriving and world leaders getting in and out. There was a clip of the President talking to the media out in the garden, the White House huge behind him.

Travis wondered what it must be like to live there – especially for a kid. Could the President's son have friends over after school? Did he have a net set up in the basement like Nish did, and could he just jump up from his homework at the kitchen table – *would he even have a kitchen table?* – and run down and take shots until, as Nish's mom always said, he'd "worked the heebie-jeebies out of his system"?

Travis knew he wouldn't trade places for anything. His father might never be on the news, people outside of Tamarack might not know his name, but he liked his quiet little house and the fact that his father worried more about things like the lawn than whether he could stop bombs from going off in the Middle East.

"You can switch it," Travis said.

Fahd fiddled with the control and the familiar Super Mario music came on. He would be lost for the next hour or so.

The telephone rang.

Travis rolled on his shoulders across the bed and dropped off the side, scooping up the phone as he fell. It was Mr. Dillinger.

"Muck wants the team down in the lobby," Mr. Dillinger said. "Round up your roomies and get everyone down here."

"Now?" Travis asked. He could see Fahd's questioning stare.

"Right now."

Muck was waiting for them, standing in the middle of the lobby with his fists jammed into his old windbreaker. He didn't seem upset, but he did look serious.

Once everyone was there, Muck began.

"The Screech Owls have been asked if they'd do a favour for our hosts," he told them. "I said I'd put it to a vote."

"What is it?" Fahd asked unnecessarily.

Muck didn't want to get to the point right away. "You know," he said, "believe it or not, Wayne Gretzky was also a peewee player much like you guys."

Travis blinked. Was Wayne Gretzky here? Was the all-time leading goal scorer in the National Hockey League coming to the tournament? Was his kid playing in it?

"Wayne Gretzky was so famous even as a peewee, he couldn't live a normal life," Muck went on. "One of the things his teammates used to do was swap jackets with him at the end of the games so he could sneak out without the other team's parents screaming at him. Did you know that?"

"Yes," said Willie Granger, the team trivia expert. No one else seemed to know.

"Mr. Dillinger and I have discussed helping out a youngster in this tournament. His team has asked us if we might consider including him in our tour plans – so he can fit in just like any other player and not be bothered by anyone."

Mr. Dillinger held out a team jacket. He'd already stitched a number on the sleeve, 17, that no one else on the team wore.

Travis felt a shiver of understanding go up and down his spine.

"Who is it?" Fahd asked.

Muck cleared his throat.

"Chase Jordan. The President's son."

"*Why us?*" Nish squeaked from the back of the gathering.

"Why not us?" Muck asked. "We're not even an American team. We're from Canada. We plan on visiting the sights. We have our own bus –"

"Even if it is only running on five cylinders," Mr. Dillinger added.

"– and, most important of all," Muck continued, "we already have a player who has to be the centre of attention everywhere he goes."

"*Who's that?*" Nish squeaked.

Muck closed his eyes and, very slightly, shook his head.

"Well?" Mr. Dillinger said. "What do we say? Do the Owls take on a temporary player or what?"

"*Yes!*" shouted Sarah.

"*Absolutely!*" yelled Sam.

"*Yes!*"

"*Yes!*"

"*Yes!*"

## 10

"YOU MIGHT NOT BELIEVE THIS," CHASE JORDAN was saying, "but I've lived here nearly two years and I've never seen the sights of Washington."

A group of the Owls were walking away from the building holding the Smithsonian space travel exhibits and back toward the park and the Washington Monument. They looked the same as always: peewee hockey players in team jackets, all of them bobbing along with their fists rammed into their windbreaker pockets.

Travis wished he could step back a moment and see if he could notice anything different about them. They were boys and girls, all around twelve years of age, some a bit bigger than others, and some standing out for other reasons – Sam's flame-coloured hair in a ponytail, Nish swaggering like he owned Washington. No one, however, would ever have noticed number 17 for anything other than the curly red hair that bounced out the back and sides of his Screech Owls ball cap.

That this was the son of the President of the United States would never have seemed possible. Wilson even wore a red maple leaf cap instead of his usual Screech Owls one so people would know this was a team from Canada. And they were sightseeing like tourists. Who would ever expect a member of the First Family, who *lived* there, to be walking around Washington gawking at the sights like he'd never been here before?

But that's how it was. The Jordans had a dog, Nixon, but even it was walked by the Secret Service. "I was surprised they didn't hook Nixon up with a plastic earplug," Chase said at one point. Travis liked him at once. He was funny. He made fun of himself. And he seemed grateful to be included as part of the gang.

Travis knew they were being watched. It made no sense just to let Chase go out wherever he wished with the Owls. Once, Travis even thought he saw Earplug himself, walking along the souvenir stands, drinking out of a water bottle and seeming to talk into his wrist as he did so. But still, they were giving Chase a little space. Fahd bought a couple of Stars-and-Stripes Frisbees and they kicked off their shoes and played on the grass in their bare feet. Willie and Fahd and Data even came up with a new game called "Frisbee hockey," and they divided up into teams, put out some runners for goal posts, and played for a good half-hour.

Chase Jordan was a good athlete. He could run almost as fast as Sarah, and he had a natural gift for throwing the Frisbee so it shot down, skimmed the ground, and then up again perfectly into another player's hands. He ran and laughed and shouted for passes, and after the first few minutes of play, it was like he'd always been an Owl.

Out of breath and damp with sweat, they broke for drinks from a little stand at the side of the road. Travis was chugging an ice-cold Snapple when he noticed Mr. Dillinger and Muck coming along from the opposite direction.

"Time you kids saw The Wall," Muck said.

"Been there, done that!" called out Nish, causing the rest of the Owls to laugh and Muck and Mr. Dillinger to look baffled. They didn't know that in Lord Stanley Public School back in Tamarack, kids who talked too much or acted up were sent to stand and face a wall to get a grip on themselves before returning to class. Some even called it "Nish's Wall" in honour of its most frequent user.

"I want you to show a little respect, Nishikawa," Muck said. "Hard as it might be for you to think about anyone but yourself, this is where you need to do it."

They began walking across the grass. Travis felt a presence at his side. He glanced over. Chase Jordan, the President's son.

"I've been a couple of times," Chase said. "But always formal things – my father speaking, that sort of thing. I always wanted to come myself but never got the chance."

Travis wasn't sure what Chase Jordan was talking about. He knew enough about Washington to know that the wall Muck was taking them to was the memorial to the Americans who had been killed in the Vietnam War. He'd seen a picture of it – rectangular black granite slabs sitting on the grass – and, to tell the truth, he hadn't been much impressed.

They could see The Wall now. It looked, from the distance, much as Travis remembered. Vertical black granite slabs banked into the grass. There was a walkway alongside it for visitors, and it was dug down so that, as the tourists walked along, the slabs rose above them and they seemed to disappear into the earth.

"*Bor-ring!*" a familiar voice hissed in Travis's ear.

"*What do we see next?*" Nish whined. "*A tree? A stick? A real, genuine stone? I can hardly wait.*"

Travis said nothing. He was afraid of being overheard by Muck or Mr. Dillinger, who were walking ahead of them each with his hands clasped in front like he was walking up the aisle in church.

Like the rest of the Owls, Travis just followed along. He let his mind drift as he began heading down the walkway.

It took a while for Travis to realize what he was passing by. First, there were just short granite slabs with a few names on them, and every now and then a date. It seemed so long ago. Nineteen fifty-eight. Nineteen sixty.

But as he began moving through the 1960s, he began to understand why it was that the walkway seemed to go down deeper into the ground. The granite slabs were rising high above him – and the number of names began growing and growing until, by the mid-1960s, he could no longer see where one year ended and the next began. There were names by the thousands. By the tens of thousands.

And then he began noticing the tributes. A small withered rose was the first that caught his attention. Someone had laid it at the foot of a slab, and he saw that there was a note attached. Travis looked in both directions. Farther along the walkway there were more flowers, some quite fresh, and more notes, and people were reading them and even photographing them. He leaned down and opened the note. It was from a woman. Her handwriting was beautiful. She had attached a picture of herself smiling and holding a small baby, a new photograph. The note was to her father. She wanted him to know that he had become a grandfather.

"I'm thirty-two now, Daddy," the note read. "Ten years older than you were when you went away forever. I would give anything to see you again for even a moment. There's someone here you should meet – Mom says he's just like you."

Travis dropped the note. He felt as if he had invaded someone's privacy. The smiling woman

and the little boy who wouldn't know his grandfather. But then, why would this woman have
put this note here if she didn't want people to
know?

Travis swallowed hard and moved on. There
were dozens of notes. There were bouquets of
flowers. He came upon an entire family – children,
parents, grandparents – taking pictures of each
other as they stood, in turn, and touched one of
the names that had been carved into the black
granite. The older people were crying, the younger
ones seemed uncertain how to react.

It was here where Travis first saw a person take
a rubbing. A woman had something that looked
like wax paper laid over one of the names and she
was rubbing furiously with what seemed to be a
thick crayon. The name was coming through onto
the paper exactly as it appeared on the granite.

He now saw that there were many people
taking rubbings. There was even a stand where
paper and crayons were being given out to anyone
who wanted them.

He was walking backwards, watching these
people, when he backed into the wheelchair.
At first, when he heard the clang and felt the
handle as he turned, he figured it would be Data.
He was already apologizing when he saw that it
wasn't Data at all. It was an old man. He had a
scraggly beard and was wearing a military shirt

with decorations over the heart. His sleeves were rolled up to reveal dark blue tattoos.

Travis knew he should have been frightened, but he wasn't. He knew the person he'd just slammed into should have been upset, but he wasn't.

"Help me out, dude?" the man asked.

Travis thought he must want to be pushed somewhere. "S-sure," he said.

The man fumbled in a bag slung from the side of his wheelchair. He pulled out some wax paper and a crayon. "I can't reach it," he said.

Travis looked into his eyes. They were clear and blue and full of pain. It took some effort to look away. The man's stare was hypnotic.

"What do you want?" Travis said.

"I need a rub to take home to Alabama," the man said in a drawl that sounded, at first, made up. "And I can't reach it, dude. You'll have to do it for me. Okay, soldier?"

Travis felt foolish being called "soldier." He was no soldier. Soldiers were tall and stood at attention like they did up at Arlington Cemetery guarding the Tomb of the Unknown Soldier. And they wore perfectly pressed uniforms, not Screech Owls jackets. And not torn and scraggly uniforms like this man wore. If he wasn't in a wheelchair, and if Travis hadn't felt sorry for him, he would have thought the man was a . . . *bum.* That's it, a bum.

"I don't know how," Travis said.

"It's not rocket science, dude," the man laughed. His teeth were black, some of them missing. "Just put the paper over the name·and rub."

Travis looked up. The names seemed to stretch into the sky.

"Which one?"

"Dougherty, C. A." the man said. "Private Charlie Dougherty."

Travis looked along the list of D's rising before him. Doyons, D. F. . . . Dover, P. L. . . . Dougherty, C. A.

"There," Travis said, pointing.

The man nodded. "My brother," he said in his deep drawl. "Not my brother in a court of law, dude, but my brother in 'Nam. We served together. I just lost my legs. He lost everything."

The man said it all so matter-of-factly it seemed unreal. Travis couldn't ask him anything more. He stretched up and started rubbing. He started with the "D" and marvelled at how it soon seemed to move off the wall and onto the paper. No wonder people wanted to take the names home with them.

Travis stretched and rubbed and the man kept talking.

"Charlie was the funniest dude you ever could imagine," he said. "They shoulda made a TV show of the things he did over there. Twice as funny as anything you ever saw on *M.A.S.H.*, I'm telling you."

Travis had to know. "What happened?"

"Charlie 'n' me and our platoon were on patrol. I stepped on a mine – last step I ever took, dude – and Charlie was the one who came back to drag me away. Carried me on his shoulders, dropped me in the medics tent and dropped dead himself. Sniper'd shot him while he was carrying me and he never even flinched. Charlie saved my life, dude – with his."

All Travis could do was nod and continue rubbing at the letters. His mind was swimming with the images this old ragged-looking man had put there: the exploding land mine, the friend running through the smoke and gunfire to rescue his buddy, knowing he'd been shot but knowing, too, he had to get back or they were both dead . . .

Travis knew nothing of war and what it could do to people. Suddenly it seemed absurd to him that, during the Stanley Cup playoffs, the announcers would talk about hockey games as though they were wars and battles. No one ever had their legs blown off in a hockey game. No one ever sacrificed his life for a teammate. There were no whistles or horns to make a war stop. War had no scoreboard.

But it did, too. It suddenly hit Travis that this was what the Vietnam memorial was all about.

It was the home-side score from a terrible war, each name a permanent loss.

He could no longer think of it as granite slabs. It was the place where this scraggly old man in the wheelchair could once again be with his buddy and thank him for what he did.

"Eighteen years old, dude – never even had a damned chance."

Travis shivered. Eighteen years old was "draft age" in hockey, an age Travis and Nish and the others sometimes dreamed they were, with their lives as NHL players just about to begin. But for Charlie Dougherty it was already over.

Travis's arms were killing him. He felt ashamed of himself. He wanted to quit because his arms hurt. Charlie Dougherty hadn't quit even after being hit by a sniper's bullet.

A big thick hand came over the top of his head and pushed against the wax paper. A second big hand reached in and took the crayon from Travis.

It was Muck.

Muck saying nothing, just reaching to take over from Travis.

Muck staring straight ahead, refusing to look down.

His big hands shaking, although he had not yet begun to rub.

## 11

TRAVIS WAS AMAZED AT HOW QUICKLY CHASE
Jordan seemed to have become best friends with
Nish. To Travis, they were direct opposites: one
red-headed, one dark; one slim, one a bit heavy;
one quiet, one loud; one seeking to escape the
spotlight, one willing to do anything for attention. But then, had he not read somewhere that
opposites attract?

By day's end, the two very different peewee
hockey players seemed lifelong buddies. They had
toured The Wall together, had played Frisbee
hockey together, and had even stuck together
when Mr. Dillinger took them all off to Dave &
Buster's, a special, three-storey extravaganza of
video games, sports fun, and restaurants. Mr.
Dillinger called it "A Special, Once-in-a-Lifetime
Stupid Stop."

They had virtual reality battles and played all
the latest video games. They ate hot dogs and
hamburgers and fries, and Nish taught Chase how
to regulate his belches after chugging an entire
Coke so he could walk along and burp loudly
every third step. During lunch, Nish told Chase

about his many adventures with plastic puke and X-ray glasses and nude beaches, and then he and Wilson taught Chase a trick they claimed they'd invented in Tamarack: cupping their palms together, squeezing out the air, and then flexing their hands to produce quick little farting sounds.

"Works great in class," Nish said as if he were giving a university lecture on the art of hand-farting. "Teachers never know who's doing it. Drives them crazy."

Chase Jordan listened intently, his eyes wide and his mouth hanging open. He mastered the "art" of hand-farting and was soon belching and burping and snorting like a Nish understudy in a play called *The Most Ignorant Twelve-Year-Old on the Face of the Earth.*

What would the President think? Travis wondered. Never mind that, he told himself. What would poor Mrs. Nishikawa think, her son corrupting the son of the President of the United States?

But he knew the truth. Mrs. Nishikawa would think it only natural that a member of the First Family would fall for the charm of her one and only darling son. And if there was trouble, she'd think it was the President's kid who had corrupted her little angel.

It hardly surprised Travis at all when Nish announced, just before the Owls all tucked in for the night, that he had struck a special deal with Chase Jordan.

"Chase's gonna pay me back for all I've done for him," Nish announced after the light was out.

Travis bit his tongue. *"All I've done for him?"* Travis repeated to himself. Where did Nish get off thinking this was all his idea?

Fahd, however, couldn't resist. "How?" he asked.

Nish lay in the dark snickering to himself.

Finally, Travis was caught. He had to know. *"How?"* he said, slightly annoyed.

Nish sighed deeply, immensely satisfied with himself.

"The Old Nisherama's gonna streak the White House."

## 12

THE SCREECH OWLS WERE PLAYING AGAIN AT THE MCI Center, but this time it was not a Swedish team from Stockholm, it was the hometown favourite, the one team that was getting all the news coverage: the Washington Wall.

"Will the President be there?" Fahd had asked on the drive over to the rink.

Mr. Dillinger had shaken his head. "He won't be there. If *I* had to choose between a hockey game and leading the Western world, I'd probably pick the hockey game – but that's why I'm not President."

"But what about the final?" Fahd persisted.

"He's supposed to come," Mr. Dillinger said, "but I doubt there's billboards up all over the world telling people not to kill each other on Sunday because the President's got to go to his kid's hockey game. If he can be there, I imagine he will. If he can't, it's no big deal."

But everything seemed like a big deal anyway. They got to the back of the rink and, again, security was everywhere, just like when they first arrived. Their bags had to be checked by the sniffer dogs, and they discovered that a strange arch had been erected just inside the door, with police tape funnelling everyone through it.

"What's that?" Lars had asked.

"Metal detector," said Data. "Same as at the airport."

One by one the Owls and their equipment went through. The players had to empty their pockets of metal and even take off their windbreakers so the zippers wouldn't set off the alarms.

Travis and Sarah were right behind Nish as he started through.

Nish was barely halfway through the detector when red lights began flashing and an alarm went off.

Instantly, there were guards everywhere.

"*Looks like it won't let a tin brain pass,*" Sarah giggled into Travis's ear.

"*Or a lead butt!*" Travis added.

But none of the security force was laughing. A stern-looking woman stepped forward. "Empty your pockets!" she ordered Nish.

Nish complied, his face reddening the deeper he dug. Candy, licorice, new gum in wrappers, old gum in Kleenex, a pen, a golf tee, coins, keys. He laid it all out in a plastic box and then the woman told him to turn around and go through again.

Again the alarm went off.

"What's in your back pocket?" the woman commanded.

"Nothin'," Nish whispered.

"There's *something* there," she snapped. "What is it?"

Nish slowly removed a long object from the back pocket of his droopy jeans.

"*What's this, then?*" she snapped.

"Remote control," Nish mumbled.

"*A what?*"

"Remote control," Nish repeated. "For a TV."

"You steal this from your hotel room, young man?"

Nish shook his head violently. "No."

"Where did you get it? Shoplifting?"

Again he shook his head. "It's mine from home."

The woman blinked several times, not comprehending. "You brought it from home," she said, a smile cracking her stern face. "What is it, your security blanket? Can't you go anywhere without television?"

"I guess," Nish said.

Travis guessed better. He remembered a conversation from the last practice before they left Tamarack. Nish had a new theory. The reason they couldn't get the adult channels in hotels, he said, was because the pay channels were all blocked through the converters.

"All I have to do is bring my own along," he had claimed. "And we'll be watching all the disgusting filth a young man needs."·

"You're sick," said Wilson.

"Why, thank you," Nish answered.

"It won't work," predicted Travis.

Nish had laughed it off, convinced he had finally solved his lifelong quest to watch restricted movies.

They finally got through the check and were on their way to the dressing room. Sarah and Travis hurried to catch up to Nish, still red-faced and sweating from the grilling he had taken.

"Well?" Travis asked. "Did it work?"

"Did what work?" Nish said, pretending not to follow.

"The remote."

Nish only shook his head angrily and hurried on, leaving Travis and Sarah to laugh at their goofy friend and try to imagine poor Mrs. Nishikawa back in Tamarack, with a solid week of searching through their little house wondering where on earth she had mislaid the television remote.

"He is a mental case," said Sarah.

"If the President only knew who his son's been hanging out with," said Travis.

## 13

"I'VE BEEN DOING SOME CALCULATIONS," MR. Dillinger was saying as he stood in the centre of the dressing room.

The Owls were all dressed for the game against the Washington Wall. Nish was in his usual pre-game pose: helmet on, head bowed down to the top of his shin pads so it looked like he was sleeping. He couldn't be, though. He was still doing that obnoxious tapping very lightly with the blade tip of his stick. *Tap-tap . . . tap-tap-tap . . . tap-tap.*

It was unusual for Mr. Dillinger to make any kind of a speech. He had a piece of paper in his hand and was checking some scribblings on it.

"Take this tournament so far," Mr. Dillinger continued. "Go back two weeks in our regular season play. Add in the tournament we played over in Parry Sound, and we're on a twelve-game unbeaten streak. Nine wins, three ties, and *zero* losses. A dozen games without a loss, Owls. That's our best streak ever!"

"Not quite," a muffled voice said from the corner.

Mr. Dillinger spun around to look at Nish, whose head was seemingly glued to his shin pads.

"*What did you say?*" Mr. Dillinger said, surprise in his voice. He began checking his figures.

"Nuthin'," the voice barely mumbled.

"No, Nish – you had something to say," Mr. Dillinger persisted.

Slowly Nish's head came up. Even through Nish's face shield Travis could see that his pal was turning beet-red.

"What was it you said?" Mr. Dillinger pressed.

Nish cleared his throat. "It's just that the *best* streak is about to come," he said in a sheepish voice.

Mr. Dillinger nodded, satisfied. "Attaboy, Nish! Thinking ahead as always. That's my boy! Win this one, and it's thirteen without a loss. Then fourteen, fifteen, sixteen . . . !"

Nish nodded happily in agreement.

Sarah and Travis looked at each other, shaking their heads in amazement.

Nish didn't mean hockey.

He was thinking of the White House.

Nish the Bubble Butt, streaking the White House.

Muck told them the tournament was running a bit late. They should keep their legs loose, the coach advised them. Loosen their skates if they liked. The delay would be at least fifteen minutes.

Some of the Owls lay flat on their backs on the floor and raised their skates up on the bench. Mr. Dillinger was a great believer in keeping the blood flowing to the brain before a big game. No one knew if this were true or not, but most of the Owls didn't want to take a chance.

Travis got up and shuffled out the door. He was too nervous to sit still. He hated delays. He always tried to finish dressing – with the sweater going over his head, him kissing the inside of it as it passed – just as Muck was coming in the door for one of his little speeches – if you could even call them that. Then they'd be up and away out the door almost immediately.

He walked along the rubber carpeting to the maintenance area. There was a swinging door there with a small window in it. On his skates, he was tall enough to look through it.

The Zamboni was already running. The driver had moved it to the entrance chute, and another worker was waiting with his hands on the lever that would open up the doors onto the chute the moment the buzzer sounded.

Travis heard the buzzer sound in the rink and a cheer from the small crowd for whichever was the winning side. Almost instantly, the worker jacked open the big doors, pushed them clear, and the Zamboni driver all but bucked the huge machine out onto the ice surface.

It had all happened in an instant. Travis was

now looking at an empty Zamboni chute.

But only empty for a moment.

As soon as the machine left, another person came in and brushed right in front of the small window Travis was staring through. It wasn't an arena worker – this was someone in a grey suit.

As Travis tried to get a second look, the grey suit shot across to the other side.

Travis jumped back.

*Earplug!*

He was moving quickly. He yanked open the door leading to the compressor and the cooling pipes, and darted in. In a moment, he was back out. He checked in closets and equipment docks and pushed aside cabinets to look behind them.

Travis shook his head. A special security sweep before a peewee hockey game when they'd already checked everyone at the entrances? The President wasn't even coming to this game.

Earplug checked to see where the Zamboni was on the ice, then pushed one of the cabinets up against the far wall, just beyond the drainage dock where the Zamboni sat when not in use.

He jumped up on the cabinet and reached above him.

Travis shook his head in amazement. Earplug was even checking the security video camera. Travis had noticed them earlier; little cameras in every corridor, panning from side to side, even outside the dressing rooms.

Earplug waited while the camera lens slowly panned away from him. Then he pulled a square block out of his jacket pocket, peeled off a paper covering that Travis realized was over sticky glue, and quickly set the block neatly into the corner of the wall so that it fit snugly and stayed there.

Travis was amazed at Earplug's thoroughness – the small block was even painted the same blue-grey colour as the walls. It was barely noticeable.

Earplug watched as the camera lens panned back towards the block, struck against it, stayed there a moment, and then reversed direction.

Earplug watched the camera move, obviously satisfied. He hopped down, quickly moving the cabinet back to its original position, and checked the camera action again. It swept across the far side of the chute, hit against the painted block, shuddered slightly, then swept back.

What was with Earplug? Travis wondered. Was he so certain something bad was going to happen in the far corner of the Zamboni chute that the camera had to do double time over that spot? A bit much, Travis figured. But then, everything to do with security and the President, and even the President's son, seemed a bit much to Travis.

He headed back to the dressing room for his stick. Earplug was already gone and the Zamboni was heading back towards the chute, the fresh new ice gleaming in the background.

## 14

TRAVIS HIT THE CROSSBAR DURING THE WARM-
up. He would have a good game. The Owls were
pumped for the match. Two of the local television stations were here to film the President's
son playing for the Wall.

"He comes one-on-one against me," Nish said
as they lined up for shots on Jenny, "I'm gonna let
him beat me."

"Is that your deal?" Sam called from the other
side of Travis. "He gets to beat you, you get to
streak his living room?"

Nish made like he was about to hurl on her.

"*Get a life!*" Sam shouted back as she jumped
up to take a shot.

"She's just jealous," Nish hissed in Travis's ear,
"'cause I'll be on TV and she won't."

The Wall were a fine team. They were coached
by a former Washington Capitals player who'd
stayed on in the area after he'd retired, and the
team played excellent positional hockey.

They did not, however, have a playmaker to
match Sarah, or anyone with quite the speed of

Dmitri. The Owls quickly went up 2–0 on a goal by Dmitri on a breakaway, and by Travis on a nice tip off a shot from the point from Sam.

Travis was impressed with Chase Jordan. He had good speed and fair skills, but more than anything else he had unbelievable determination. He was the kind of player Muck liked best, the player who can deliver a better game than his skills would suggest, simply out of sheer will.

It took a while for the Washington Wall to find their game. They seemed intimidated by the Owls at first, but by the second period they had come to realize if they put a special checker – Chase Jordan – on Sarah, they could do much to neutralize the Owls.

"He's good," Sarah puffed as their line came off for a break.

Travis nodded. He heard the admiration in Sarah's voice. She was different from most other good players, who showed their frustration at being checked. Sarah never got angry. She got even. She would figure out Chase Jordan.

The Wall tied the game at 3–3 and then went ahead 4–3 on a fluke goal that went in off Fahd's skate.

Chase Jordan went off for tripping on the next shift, however, after hauling down Sarah when she gave him the slip. The cameras were right on him during the play and followed him into the penalty box. Travis was certain this would be the clip they'd be playing on the evening news.

"She shoulda got a penalty herself for diving," Nish hissed as he and Travis circled, killing time before the faceoff.

Travis couldn't believe what he was hearing. Nish was blaming Sarah for faking the trip, just so she could get on television instead of him.

Travis could sense what was coming. Nish was going "coast-to-coast" the second he got the puck. Nish knew that if the Owls scored while the President's son was in the penalty box, it would become part of the story.

Sarah won the faceoff and sent the puck over to Travis, who chipped it back to Nish.

Nish turned back, leaving the checkers waiting. He went behind his own net, stickhandling slowly, and stopped.

Ridiculous, Travis thought. It looked to the crowd like Nish was figuring out the lay of the ice, but in fact all he was doing was waiting for the cameras to find him.

Satisfied, Nish began stickhandling out of his own end. Up to the blueline and over, where the first checker tried for him.

Nish faked a pass to Travis. The checker fell for it, and Nish stepped around him, moving to centre.

A second checker charged, but Nish deftly slipped the puck between the Wall player's skates and picked it up on the other side.

Dmitri was breaking fast, pounding the ice for the pass that should have come.

But Nish wasn't passing.

Dmitri broke over the line offside, braked so hard snow flew up towards the glass, and he cut back hard, straddling the blueline with one leg while he waited to see what Nish would do.

Nish changed speeds, moving quickly toward the blueline. The Wall defence backpedalled, moving in towards him to pinch him off if necessary.

Sarah was clear on the other side, but Nish ignored her.

Travis looped back, coming in behind Nish for the drop pass, but Nish ignored him.

Nish let the puck go, raised his arms, and drove like a bulldozer into the two defenders as all three came together. Both Wall defence went down, leaving Nish staggering slightly but still moving.

He raced for the puck just as the Wall goaltender decided to lunge for it with his stick.

Nish reached out at the same moment, and the puck popped between the two stick blades, rising high and spinning until it came down on the far side of the net.

Sarah was there, waiting.

The goalie sprawled helplessly as Sarah came in on the empty net. She tapped the puck in and spun into Dmitri's arms.

Tie game, 4–4!

All the Owls on the ice converged on Sarah, slapping her helmet and pounding her on the back. All but Nish, who lightly tapped her shin pads and spun away.

"Glory hog!" he hissed back.

The Owls moved ahead to stay on a sweet goal by Simon, a hard blast by Andy, and a weird "knuckler" from the blueline by Wilson.

The clock was ticking down fast, with the Owls ahead 7–4, when, in the dying moments, Chase Jordan swept the puck away from Sarah and ended up all alone with it at centre ice.

Sarah had fallen when Chase Jordan checked her, so she was out of the play. Dmitri and Travis were too far down the ice to get back in time. Fahd, the other Owls defence, was out of position and scrambling to get back.

It was Chase Jordan against Nish. One on one.

Chase Jordan came over the blueline, with only Nish between him and the net. He set to shoot, no doubt hoping to blast a screen shot that Jenny wouldn't see until too late.

Nish fell to block the shot, spinning towards Chase.

Chase seemed surprised – Nish had gone down too soon.

He checked his swing and drew the puck back again with his blade, out of Nish's reach.

Nish spun helplessly towards the boards.

Chase moved in quickly. Forehand, backhand, forehand, backhand again.

Jenny went for the fake, guessing.

Chase held, the side of the net opening up.

He looped a high backhand in under the crossbar, sending the water bottle sailing as high as if Dmitri himself had taken the shot.

The horn blew. The whistle blew. The Wall bench emptied, every player charging Chase Jordan for his spectacular goal.

The cameras were racing out onto the ice.

Forget the penalty, forget the girl the President's son had tripped – *this* was the shot for the evening news! The Owls had won 7–5, but anyone who walked into the building at that moment would think the Wall had won the Stanley Cup.

The Owls each rapped Jenny's pads and then lined up to shake hands with the Wall who were still celebrating.

Travis found himself lining up right behind Nish. He couldn't help but ask. "You *didn't*, did you?"

Nish turned, face red, eyes wide. "*What?*" Nish asked, as if he had no clue what Travis meant.

"Let him do that?"

Nish grinned, ear to ear. "What do you take me for?"

Travis couldn't be bothered answering.

It would take forever.

## 15

TRAVIS WOKE TO THE SOUND OF FAHD CLICKING through the television channels in search of car-toons.

*Click.*

"Shoot!"

*Click.*

"Bor-ring!"

*Click.*

"Dumb!"

*Click.*

"It should be illegal to run news on Saturday mornings!"

Travis rolled over, rubbing the sleep out of his eyes and trying to focus on the rapidly flipping television screen. Fahd was right. Saturday morning in Washington, D.C., and it seemed every television station was talking about the big crisis they were trying to solve at the White House. Channel after channel showed nothing but men in blue suits talking. A spokesman from the White House was saying they were this close – and he held out his thumb and forefinger with a tiny gap between them – from reaching a breakthrough

69

agreement. No one knew what would happen, but that wasn't stopping every expert on television from giving an opinion.

Travis agreed with Fahd. He'd rather watch cartoons.

"This is *ridiculous!*" said Fahd, slamming down the remote.

Travis was about to suggest they pass on cartoons and play a round of Nintendo instead, when the telephone rang beside Nish's bed.

A huge pillow looped over from the other side and smothered the phone. Nish's way of answering.

Lars dug out the phone and answered it. "Johanssen."

Travis shook his head. He'd never heard anyone answer a telephone that way until Lars came over from Sweden. Lars said he couldn't understand why people in North America just answered "Hello," and he refused to change.

"Uh huh . . . yeah . . . uh huh . . . okay . . . thanks." He hung up.

Travis waited, but Lars wasn't quick enough. "*What?*" Travis and Fahd said at once.

"Mr. Dillinger. Chase Jordan's pulled a few strings, it seems."

"*Meaning?*" Fahd said, again not waiting for Lars to finish.

"*Our White House tour starts in forty-five minutes!*" Fahd pumped a fist. "*Yes!*"

On Nish's bed, several pillows shifted. A huge, puzzled face emerged, like a bear shaking off a cover of snow.

"*Huh?*" Nish grunted.

"*The tour! Nish! We got the tour!*"

"*Whazzat?*" Nish mumbled.

"*We're going to the White House!*"

Nish shook his head again, rubbed a hand through his flyaway hair, then began nodding and smiling.

"You gotta get ready," Fahd said, scrambling to put on his Owls track pants.

"We've only got forty-five minutes," added Lars.

With a big arm, Nish swept away the remaining pillows and sheets that were covering him.

He was buck-naked, not a stitch on.

"*I'm already ready!*"

●

They made it easily. Mr. Dillinger had the bus rolled up to the hotel entrance and the Owls hurried out and into their seats for the short ride over to the White House. They were all in their team windbreakers, Nish included. They had on their Owls track pants, Nish included. He'd even taken time to comb his unruly hair. They looked like a perfect, well-behaved peewee hockey team, which is exactly what they were – with one possible exception. But Travis wasn't that worried about Nish. He wouldn't have the nerve to try anything stupid here.

Chase Jordan had made wonderful arrangements. A tour guide met their bus and took them in through a special entrance. With the Summit underway, most of the White House had been cordoned off to the usual tour groups, but there were still parts of the enormous building open to the public, and the Owls were going to see other rooms in the White House that visitors rarely see.

Chase Jordan high-fived the Owls as he joined them for the tour. He was wearing his Washington Wall track pants and a Capitals T-shirt.

The guide was great. She told stories about the history of the White House, and even one wild story about a child ghost – a young son of Abraham Lincoln who had died there – who people claimed to have seen over the past century and more. She took them through the portrait gallery and showed them various rooms – including the Lincoln bedroom, where rich tourists were allowed to pay to stay over. No one seemed more pleased with the tour than Muck, the history lover. Chase Jordan added the odd story from the present. He even showed them his secret hall, where he and his brother sometimes played hockey mini-sticks below the glowering portraits of Herbert Hoover and George Washington.

"We're going now to see the Oval Office," the guide told them. "That's where the President does most of his work."

"Is he there now?" Fahd asked.

The guide shook her head, smiling. "No. I'm afraid not. There are special meetings going on in the West Wing, where we won't be allowed today. They might prove to be the most important meetings in the world this year. So you're lucky to be here on such a historic occasion."

"Fantastic!" Sam said. "We get to be a part of history!"

Travis felt Sarah nudging his arm. She had a worried look on her face.

"What is it?" he whispered.

"Have you seen Nish?"

Travis looked around.

No Nish, anywhere.

"I think I saw him and Chase slip through that door back there," Sarah whispered as quietly as she could.

Travis squeezed his eyes shut and shook his head violently.

Surely not.

*Anything* but that.

## 16

MUCK AND MR. DILLINGER WERE SO WRAPPED up in the tour of the White House that neither was aware that a Screech Owl had gone missing.

Travis felt sick to his stomach. Normally, if one of the players was missing, there would be an instant alert and they would all go off and try to find the straggler. But this wasn't normal. This was Nish, and he was with the President's son. They were in the White House, Chase Jordan's own home. So it was hardly as if Nish was *lost*.

Maybe Nish had just gone to the bathroom or something. That would be perfectly normal: Chase taking Nish off to a washroom in another part of the White House.

But he didn't believe it. And he knew, as captain, he should let Muck or Mr. Dillinger know if something was wrong.

They spent about fifteen minutes in the spectacular Oval Office. They saw the chair where President Kennedy had sat. They were told that here was where the critical decisions had been made for every war America had fought – including both world wars and the Vietnam

War – and here was where the famous tapes had been made that caught President Nixon in a lie and led to his resignation in disgrace.

The tour of the Oval Office over, they headed out through a corridor towards the garden, where the President held so many of his press conferences. Just as Travis decided now was the time to tell Muck and Mr. Dillinger, a door swung open and Nish and Chase Jordan spilled through.

Both looked like they'd seen a ghost.

"Where *were* you guys?" Fahd asked.

"Nowhere," Nish said quickly.

"Washroom," Chase Jordan said. "Nish isn't feeling well."

That explains Nish's look, Travis thought. But what about Chase? He looked just as shocked. They couldn't both have been ill, could they?

"Something's happened," Sarah whispered to Travis.

Nish was uncommonly quiet on the bus ride back to the hotel. No farting noises, no burping or belching or screaming at the top of his lungs. No irritating *tap-tap . . . tap-tap-tap . . . tap-tap* on the window. Just Nish sitting quietly near the front of the bus, his hands folded in his lap as he stared out like an elderly tourist interested in the architecture of downtown Washington.

Something *had* happened. Travis just wasn't sure he wanted to know what.

## 17

THEY HAD TWO HOURS TO KILL BEFORE HEADING off for the next game, this one against the Portland Panthers, the team the Owls had come up against in so many other tournaments.

Muck told them they could take a nap in their rooms or go for a walk around the block, but nothing energetic and no straying too far.

Travis tried to doze off a while. Fahd began flipping once again through the TV channels.

*Click.*

"Darn!"

*Click.*

"Stupid!"

*Click.*

"*Gimmee that!*" someone screamed out.

It was Nish, his hand shaking as he reached out and demanded the remote from Fahd.

"GIVE IT TO ME!" Nish shouted.

"Okay, okay," Fahd said, flipping it to him.

Nish jammed it into his belt. "You watch way too much television, you know," he said angrily.

"And *you* don't?" Fahd asked.

"Muck wants you to get ready for the game," Nish said, his face beaming red. "Think about that, not some stupid cartoons."

With the remote control still jammed in his belt, Nish walked out and slammed the door.

Nish had never gone for a walk in his life. He adored cartoons. And since when had noise ever bothered him?

"I don't understand," said Lars.

"There's something he doesn't want us to know," suggested Travis.

"Or *see*," added Fahd.

"What do you mean?" Travis asked.

"He took the remote," Fahd said. "It can't be just to stop me watching cartoons."

"Then why?" asked Lars.

"So *we* couldn't watch," said Travis. "There's something on TV that's bothering him."

"Let's check it out," said Fahd.

"We *can't*!" Lars said, shaking his head in disbelief. "He took the control – remember?"

Fahd giggled. "I know he took it," he said. "But don't forget he also *brought* one."

The TV remote from home! The one that was supposed to get Nish access to those movies he was always trying to see.

"Where is it?" Lars demanded.

"In his equipment bag," Fahd said.

All three looked at each other.

"I'm not sticking my hand in there!" said Fahd.

"We need one of those dogs!" laughed Lars.

"C'mon," said Travis. "Somebody's got to do it."

They gathered over Nish's hockey bag like they were about to defuse a bomb. Travis quickly unzipped the bag.

"*Open the window!*" Fahd called.

"I'll get it!" Lars said, glad for an excuse to back away.

Travis held his nose and reached his free hand in, moving it about quickly. His imagination raced with wild ideas: tarantulas, lizards, rattlesnakes, rotting corpses, slugs, horse droppings . . .

"It might not be so bad," Fahd said in a calm voice. "Everything's fairly fresh since they blew up his other bag."

Travis groped around, then felt something that was either a rock-hard chocolate bar or the remote. He pulled it out.

*Mrs. Nishikawa's missing remote!*

"I'm surprised the plastic didn't melt," said Lars.

Travis aimed Mrs. Nishikawa's remote at the television and pushed "power." The television clicked, hissed, then brightened. He pushed the channel button.

*Click.*

A nature show.

*Click.*

News.

*Click.*

78

More news.

"It's the same old junk!" Fahd whined. "There's nothing here about the hockey team."

Lars seemed unconvinced. "If there's nothing on but news," he said, "maybe it's the news he doesn't want us watching."

Travis clicked over to CNN, the all-news channel. There were more reports from the White House. Then more political experts. Then reports from the countries involved in the Summit.

"*Bor-ring!*" Fahd called out every so often.

"A few more minutes," said Lars. He seemed to be losing hope himself.

The news anchor was smiling now.

"A most unusual development today at the White House Summit," she said. "We go now to Andrew Carter for a report."

The three boys watched as the picture turned to a CNN reporter standing just in front of the White House.

"White House staff have been scrambling since before noon to explain the circumstances behind today's bizarre developments at the Summit . . ."

The screen switched to stock shots of the Summit: mostly men talking to other men, men meeting in corridors, men gathered around a long table.

"Around 10:45, according to witnesses, a door to the boardroom where the main Summit participants had gathered burst open, and what appeared to be a naked young man wearing only a hockey goaltender's mask ran into the room, stopped sharply, and ran right back out . . .

"Both sides have accused the other of deliberately trying to sabotage the Summit with this unusual incident . . .

"CNN has obtained amateur videotape of the incident taken by one of the participating officials. We apologize for the poor quality, but it does give some sense of what occurred late this morning at the White House . . ."

The screen went fuzzy, a lens moved in and out of focus. The video was of poor quality, as warned, but clearly showed men gathering in a room and sitting down. Then the picture jumped and blurred across the room to catch only the hasty exit of the young man.

A young man wearing nothing but a goalie mask, his big, naked bum churning out the door.

"I'd recognize that butt anywhere," said Lars, shaking his head.

Travis closed his eyes, hoping it would go away. When he opened them the film was being run again. Nish's naked butt, *on instant replay!*

CNN switched back to the reporter, who was doing his best not to smile.

"Early reports were that this was a prank pulled off by the President's hockey-loving son, Chase, but the White House has strongly denied that the naked youngster is Chase Jordan . . .

"The White House has assured Summit participants that an immediate investigation will be carried out and, once identified, the guilty party will issue an apology. The incident is being treated as a scandal in parts of the Middle East, where public streaking is not considered quite as humorous as it might be here in North America. The President, according to sources, is furious over the incident and fearful that it may derail the agreement he had hoped could be reached today."

Travis flicked the channel.

More news on the White House streaker. More videotape replay.

Another channel, one more shot of the streaker.

"That's our teammate," Lars said.

"Internationally famous," added Fahd, "just like he always wanted."

## 18

"*VERY FUNNY!*"

Jeremy Weathers's goal mask went flying across the room and slammed into the far wall.

There wasn't a Screech Owl in the room not howling with laughter. Well, there was one. Wayne Nishikawa, CNN headline news, the "butt" of every joke in America.

"I just wanted you to know where you were sitting," Jeremy called back to Nish as he scrambled to pick up his goalie mask.

"I *know* where I'm sitting!" Nish snarled.

"*Right on the most famous big butt in America!*" Sam roared, and the dressing room howled once more with laughter.

The President had issued immediate apologies to each participant in the Summit, and they had been accepted. The Summit was once again underway.

The President had even answered questions about the incident at his daily press conference, but most of the questions ended in giggles, and even the President couldn't help but laugh a few times.

"When I declared my candidacy for President,"

he said with a straight face, "there were people on the other side who said they didn't want a bum in the White House."

The White House press gallery groaned at the bad joke, and that appeared to be it for the infamous "White House Streaker," as Nish had become known all over the world.

Only no one knew it was Nish. The Owls knew, and probably Muck and Mr. Dillinger knew, but all the reports had blamed it on one of the President's rambunctious kids, and Chase, to his great credit, had said nothing to set the record straight.

Nish would neither confirm nor deny that he was the White House Streaker.

"You really think there's another butt like that in the world?" Sam had asked.

"He had a mask on!" Nish protested.

"His face," Sarah said, "is not important. Put that butt of yours in a police lineup and anybody would pick you out."

"Sit on it!" Nish snapped.

Mr. Dillinger came whistling through the door, carrying his portable skate sharpener. He set it up in a corner, plugged it in, and began work on some skates.

No one spoke above the grinding whine of the machine as Mr. Dillinger expertly drew skates back and forth over the stone, the sparks shooting out behind like a miniature comet's tail.

Muck came in just as the last Owls were fastening their helmets tight. He stood in the middle of the room and stared hard at Nish.

Nish looked up once, then went back to his pre-game ritual of laying his head down over the tops of his shin pads. Travis could still see that his friend was redder than usual.

Muck said nothing. He turned and looked at all the players, one after the other.

"You know this team," he said. "Portland's a great side. They have size and speed. Look out for the big centre, Sarah. They're hurting, though. The little defenceman – I forget his name –"

"Billings," Travis said. He still had the signed card he'd exchanged with the little defenceman back in Lake Placid.

"Billings," Muck continued. "He's out with an ankle sprain. He won't be dressing."

Travis felt a twinge of regret. He knew what Billings meant to the Panthers. He also knew that not having him on the ice would help the Owls considerably, but he considered the little Portland defender a friend even though they barely knew each other.

"One more thing," Muck said. "We win this game, we're in the finals."

It was all Muck needed to say. The Screech Owls played as if possessed. Sarah was exceptional, shutting down Yantha, the big Portland centre, and scoring twice herself. Dmitri scored one of his "flying water bottle" specials, and Nish scored a beauty on an end-to-end rush.

The Panthers clearly missed Billings. With no one to get the puck out of their end or make the long pass, they weren't nearly the team they should have been, and the Owls won easily, 6−2, with Sam and Derek scoring late in the game.

Travis had three assists and felt terrific. He knew, however, that all the glory went to the goal scorers. Perhaps he and Muck would be the only two who had noticed how well he had played.

They lined up to shake hands. The Panthers were on the verge of elimination. Either they won their next game or they were headed home.

Travis went down the line, bumping gloves with the various Panthers, including big Yantha.

He was about to turn away and head for the exit when he noticed one more player coming to shake hands. It was Billings, limping badly, an upturned hockey stick for a crutch as he made his way across the ice.

He was smiling. "I gave you first star, Travis."

Travis high-fived the open hand presented to him.

"Thanks," Travis said.

"See you next tournament."

Travis nodded.

Someone else had noticed.

## 19

MOST OF THE OTHER OWLS HAD ALREADY HEADED for the team bus for the ride back to the hotel when Travis, Fahd, Lars, and Nish decided to take the shortcut out the Zamboni chute and through the back door.

They were just moving into the Zamboni chute when a familiar voice barked, *"Halt! Who goes there?"*

*Earplug!*

They couldn't see him, but they could hear him. "What is this?" Nish said. "A *pirate* movie?"

Travis cringed. The old Nish was back – but this was hardly the time to kid around.

*"Identify yourselves immediately!"* Earplug barked.

"T–Travis Lindsay," Travis said.

"Fahd Noorizadeh."

"Lars Johanssen."

"Paul Kariya."

Travis winced.

*"Drop the bags!"* the voice ordered.

The four Owls dropped their equipment bags.

*"Up against the wall!"*

The four boys moved towards the wall. Nish, having seen it so many times on television, automatically faced the wall and leaned against it, his hands high, as if he were about to be frisked.

Earplug came around the doorway, his hand tucked inside his jacket like it was petting his revolver.

"*That's the idea, Kariya!*" he called out. "*You others do the same!*"

The three followed Nish's lead, Fahd letting a giggle slip out as he did so. *Kariya?*

"*What's so funny, you?*" Earplug snapped.

"Nothing," Fahd said in a quick, small voice.

"*What are you boys doing here? This is a restricted zone!*"

"*We're taking a shortcut, sir!*" Nish barked back, as if he were a marine recruit.

This time both Fahd and Lars giggled. Let it alone, Nish, Travis thought. Let it alone.

"Shortcut?" Earplug said, for the first time speaking in a nearly normal voice.

"The team bus is out back," Travis said. "We always go through this way. It's shorter."

"You'll go through this way no more, young man," Earplug said. "The FBI and Secret Service have declared this off limits to the end of the tournament. *Understand?*"

"*Yessss, sirrrrr!*" Nish snapped back over his shoulder.

"You other boys act more like Kariya, here," said Earplug. "And we'll understand each other just fine. Now get out of here, the *long* way!"

"*Yessss, sirrrrr!*" Nish snapped again.

The four Owls gathered up their equipment bags and sticks and turned back the way they'd come, heading the long way around for the bus. Mr. Dillinger and Muck would be wondering what had happened to them.

"What's with the 'Paul Kariya'?" Lars asked Nish as they went through a door into the corridor heading toward the front entrance.

"First thing that came into my mind," Nish said.

Travis shook his head. Life would certainly be a lot easier if only his friend would wait for the second, third, fourth – *or two hundredth* – thing that came into his twisted mind.

## 20

"CHASE'S TEAM BEAT THE PANTHERS!" LARS shouted.

Travis couldn't believe it. The Washington Wall beat the Portland Panthers? *Impossible.* But then he remembered – Billings still hadn't been able to play. Without him, the Panthers were just another team. And now they were out of the tournament.

"*The final's at six o'clock!*" Fahd yelled. "*We're playing the Washington Wall for the championship!*"

"And they've just announced that the President *can* come!" added Lars.

There'd be more television coverage than the Owls had ever experienced.

All the Owls but one, that is.

One of them – or at least a significant *part* of one of them – was already a television star around the world.

Entering the MCI Center later in the afternoon was like entering an armed camp. The Owls had been amazed before by the security when Chase Jordan was playing, but that was nothing compared to this.

There were Secret Service men everywhere. There were metal detectors and X-ray machines and guards at every entrance and, once again, dogs to check every equipment bag.

"Good thing they don't have sniffer dogs for streakers' bums!" Sam yelled out.

"*Shut up!*" Nish snapped, his face glowing like the burner on a stove.

They're going too far with Nish, Travis thought. I've got to put a stop to this.

But there was no time. The delay getting into the rink meant that they had to hurry into their hockey equipment, and Mr. Dillinger was in the dressing room sharpening a few of the Owls' skates. There was no use trying to talk over the noise.

Nish had dressed in silence and was sitting in his usual corner in his usual fashion: head down on the tops of his shin pads, his eyes closed. Normally, Travis would have thought his friend was trying to "envision" the upcoming match, but this time he had the feeling that Nish was trying to escape.

The machine shut off.

I should say something, Travis thought. I should do it now.

But he was too late. Willie and Andy and Wilson were already back at it.

"Can you imagine if they *did* have a sniffer dog for streakers!" Wilson shrieked, still laughing at Sam's joke.

"*No dog'd take the job!*" giggled Willie.

"*It'd be worse than getting skunked!*" laughed Andy.

Nish's head was up. He looked furious.

He stood up, and with a swift kick of one skate, sent all the sticks flying off the wall in Andy's direction.

"*Hey!*" Mr. Dillinger shouted.

But Nish was already at the door and out, slamming it hard behind him.

Should I go after him? Travis wondered. No. Give him a minute or two by himself. Deal with the team first.

"Lay off him, okay?" Travis said.

"It's just a little fun," Andy said weakly.

"I know," Travis said. "But fun's over. Can't you see he's had enough?"

No one said anything. Travis was afraid they thought he was being too pushy, that he was overreacting.

"He's right," Sarah said. "Let's just let it go."

Travis felt the air come out of his lungs. He hadn't realized how tightly he'd been holding his breath. Thank heavens for Sarah.

"He's still a butt brain," Sam said.

I can't argue with that, Travis thought. But he wisely said nothing.

## 21

NISH BURST THROUGH THE DRESSING-ROOM door, slammed it behind him, and instantly wondered why he'd done it. He didn't know which way to go. *Back into the dressing room? Take off somewhere? Wait where he was until Muck came along?*

He had that old out-of-control feeling inside him, almost as if his blood was boiling and steaming through his veins. He could still remember how, whenever he got this way when he was small – frustrated, angry, upset, his brain spinning, racing – his mother would simply pick him up, hold his arms tight to his body, and move somewhere quiet with him until he calmed down. He wished his mother was here right now. But she wouldn't be able to pick him up any more. And she might find out he'd run off with the television remote . . .

He tried counting to ten. He tried holding his breath. He tried counting back from ten. He needed to move. He needed to shake the hot blood out of his veins and the spiders out of his stomach and the squirrels out of his head. If he didn't move, he thought he'd explode.

Careful not to scrape his skates, Nish shuffled down the corridor towards the Zamboni chute just as Muck came around the far corner from the opposite direction.

Muck stared curiously at Nish. No one, not even Mrs. Nishikawa, understood Wayne Nishikawa better than Muck Munro, the coach of the Screech Owls. He'd known Nish for too long now. He'd seen him in every imaginable state of mind, including the one where he just had to get away and be on his own.

Muck decided to let him go, for the time being.

Travis had his head down, thinking about the game, when Muck came into the dressing room. Muck looked his usual self: casual, relaxed, more like he was about to go fishing than coach a team in a championship game. A championship game before the President of the United States.

Travis couldn't stop a small smile from flickering across his face. Most coaches would have worn a suit under the circumstances. Most would be carrying a clipboard filled with nonsense, or chewing ice like they do in the NHL. But not Muck. Never Muck. Same old windbreaker. Same old pants. Same old boots.

"Nishikawa needs some private time," Muck said matter-of-factly.

"We kidded a bit too much," Sarah said.

Good for Sarah, Travis thought. If he had said it, it would have sounded more like "telling."

"He'll be fine," Muck said.

"When're we on?" Fahd asked.

"Zamboni's finished," Muck said. "We can go out any time."

The Screech Owls started moving, but Muck held up his hand, palm out, and they stopped dead.

"A couple of things."

Travis sat back, slightly surprised. Muck rarely talked to them before games, and most assuredly *never* gave anything like a "coach's speech."

"They're a good team," Muck said. "You already know that. They tied you in the early round. They're very well coached and play exceptional positional hockey. But they do make mistakes. We stay in our positions and trust in their mistakes. When they make one, we pounce with our speed. Okay?"

"Okay," Fahd said unnecessarily.

"Now there's a lot of attention out there. Cameras. Reporters. Lots of people. They're not here to see you. They're here because the President's coming later and the President's kid is playing. I don't want anybody thinking outside the ice surface, okay?"

"Okay," Fahd said.

"I don't know why I'm telling you all this," Muck smiled. "The only one I really need to speak to isn't even here."

Nish could feel himself calming down. The squirrels were slowing in his head. The spiders were quiet in his gut. His blood was flowing rather than boiling over. Even his thoughts were back as close to normal as they ever got.

He just needed some space. Just a little time to himself and he could go back and join the team like everything was back to the way it used to be. If they said nothing, he'd say nothing. They could all just forget any of this stupid stuff ever happened.

Nish figured he needed something to distract himself. Something else to think about apart from Sam's constant cracks and what might happen if the authorities found out he was the one who streaked the President.

The Zamboni room. He'd go in and check it out. Maybe talk to the driver about keeping ice down here in Washington where it could get so hot at this time of year. Something to take his mind off everything.

Nish stood at the door and tried to see into the Zamboni chute area, but the window in the door was papered over for some reason, as if they were trying to keep people out. Or at least from seeing in.

Nish knew the Zamboni driver wouldn't mind. He was a happy old guy, always laughing and joking with the kids. Nish would just walk in and start talking to him. He leaned into the door.

The door opened too fast – almost as if someone had yanked it from the other side. Nish fell through the doorway, his skates scraping horribly across the concrete floor.

He felt something being slapped over his mouth just as he opened it to cry out. Something sticky – and terrible-tasting!

*Duct tape!*

And then pain – followed by darkness.

There was a quick knock on the dressing-room door and a man's voice called out. "*Ice's ready! You're on, Screech Owls!*"

Muck checked his watch and shrugged. "I guess Nish is having a longer talk with himself than I thought," he said. "He'll just have to catch up to us. *Let's go!*"

"*Yesss!*" shouted Sam.

"*Go Owls!*" called Sarah.

"*Be smart!*" Travis yelled.

"*Go Can-a-da!!*" shouted Fahd.

## 22

TRAVIS HIT THE CROSSBAR FIRST SHOT IN THE warm-up. He felt good. The ice was in perfect shape. The rink was filled with far more fans than the usual crowd of parents and relatives. There were several TV crews as well, but none of the cameras was pointed in the direction of the Owls. All media attention was on the Washington Wall, Chase Jordan's team.

Mr. Dillinger had found out that the President would be arriving around the third period. It was all he could manage with his busy schedule, especially with the White House Summit about to wind up. He'd watch the final period and then make the presentation.

Travis didn't doubt for a moment that the crowd would be cheering for the Wall. Especially the television people. Footage of the President handing the trophy to his own son would be far more valuable than shots of the President of the United States shaking hands with some little kid from Canada.

It made Travis want to win all the more.

The officials were calling the teams to get ready for the faceoff. Travis looked desperately towards the door leading to the dressing rooms.

Still no sign of Nish.

Muck seemed equally concerned. He whispered something to Mr. Dillinger just before the opening faceoff, and Mr. Dillinger hopped over the boards at the visitors' bench and headed back through the seats towards the exit.

He would be going to get Nish.

Everything would be all right.

The squirrels in Nish's head and the spiders in his gut were gone, but now that he had come to, he had howling hyenas up top and crocodiles below. He was terrified he would throw up. With duct tape covering his mouth, he'd choke himself and *die*!

He couldn't see. He couldn't yell.

He couldn't move his hands. They must be wrapped in duct tape, too.

He had no idea where he was. It was cold and hard and damp, that was all he knew.

Perhaps it was the cameras, perhaps it was knowing the President of the United States was going to be there – whatever it was, the Owls were off their game and the Wall were on theirs.

The Washington team seemed driven to play hard. Maybe it was the idea of beating the

Canadians at their national game. Or maybe they were just more used to all the attention that came from having Chase Jordan on their team.

Chase scored the first goal on a beautiful passing play with one of his wingers. They forced a turnover on Andy's line and came in so fast that Willie Granger failed to get back in time, stranding Fahd to deal with the attack.

Chase hit his left wing early with a pass, Fahd went for the puck carrier, the winger flipped the puck back, and Chase one-timed it behind Jeremy.

Travis cringed on the bench. Fahd should never have fallen for it. Nish would have stayed to the middle, taking away the pass and letting them have the long shot if they wanted.

*Where was he?*

## 23

METAL, NISH THOUGHT.

Whatever he was on, it was metal. And *tight*, an enclosed space.

He tapped one skate against the wall to make sure. Hard, cold, wet metal. But what was it, and where was it, and why was he there?

Nish tried to piece together what little he knew.

What had he heard? *Nothing*. He'd pushed through the door, and the door had seemed to fall away. In an instant, he'd been down on the floor and the tape was ripping and then it was over his mouth and then everything went dark.

What had he seen?

*Nothing.*

Chase Jordan was having the game of his life. He'd scored twice and set up another by the time the first period was over. The Washington Wall were ahead 4–2. Only Sarah, on a backhand as she'd been tripped, and Jesse, on a wraparound that caught the Wall goaltender off guard, had been able to score for the Owls.

Travis knew what was wrong. The Wall were sending two forecheckers in hard to try to panic the Owls' defence, while the third forward, usually the centre, stayed back around the blueline ready to pounce on any long passes the panicking Owls defence might try.

Travis also knew what was missing.

If Nish were on the ice, the Wall wouldn't have been getting nearly so many chances. Nish knew how to get a puck out of his own end. He could carry a puck better than anyone but Sarah, and he had a good eye for the long breakaway pass to Dmitri or Travis on the wings. He also knew how to defend in his own end.

Travis had already seen Mr. Dillinger come back shaking his head, and he had caught the look on Muck's face as the coach realized Nish was nowhere to be found.

*So where was he?* Travis asked himself. How badly had they hurt Nish's feelings? Could he have left the rink?

No. He'd left his clothes and runners in the dressing room when he stomped out. Travis tried to imagine Nish, in full equipment, scraping along Pennsylvania Avenue, in his skates, around the Washington Monument and the long reflecting pool while office workers sat about in the sun.

Travis knew Nish had to be in the MCI Center. *But where?*

## 24

THE THIRD PERIOD WAS UNDERWAY, WITH THE Wall ahead 5–4. Chase Jordan had scored his third goal of the game, and there had been a delay while a couple of dozen hats soared out of the stands and onto the ice to celebrate the hat-trick. The cameras had recorded every moment of it, even coming down onto the ice to film the workers piling the hats into a large garbage bag.

It seemed to Travis that nothing could stop the Washington Wall. Everything seemed to be working out for everyone: Chase was having the game of his life; the Wall were leading in the championship game; and the television crews were delighted with their story. All that was needed to complete the perfect day was for the President to arrive and present the trophy to his own son.

Perfect, Travis thought, for everyone but the Screech Owls. They weren't on their game. He liked Chase Jordan enough to appreciate what this must mean to him, but he couldn't help but feel that this was not a true measure of the Owls.

They needed their top defenceman. Desperately.

But there was no sign of Nish. No word. Nothing.

Nish had never tasted anything so horrible. He was chewing the duct tape from the inside. His mouth must have been opened to scream when the tape was slapped over it. He could move his jaw just enough to bite into the tape and grind at it.

It tasted bad. But it was working. He had chewed a small hole in the cover, but not enough yet to call for help. All he could manage was a tiny squeak.

He thought he could hear something now, but the sounds were terribly muffled. He felt like he was inside a cookie tin. Some container of some kind. And somewhere beyond the cold metal walls was the sound of a crowd calling and cheering. He also thought he heard a buzzer.

*He must still be inside the rink!*

He chewed faster and harder.

Two minutes to go, and the Owls were still down by a goal. Muck called Sarah's line out for the faceoff, and Travis leapt the boards, tapping Andy's and Jesse's shin pads as they puffed by to take their rest on the bench. All the Owls were giving everything they had, but it was doing no good. They needed someone to move that puck up.

They circled for the faceoff, Sarah choking up on her stick as she began to glide in for the puck drop. Suddenly there was a huge commotion in the crowd, and the linesman backed off, waiting.

Everyone in the rink, players included, turned their attention to an entrance to the stands.

An army of Secret Service men, led by Earplug, were moving down the aisle towards a seat just behind the Wall's bench.

Earplug seemed even more nervous than usual. His eyes were darting every which way. His hand was tucked inside his jacket, ready at any moment to pull out his gun.

To Travis, it seemed unbelievable. More like a movie than real life. But then the stands broke into applause and cheers. Behind the first wave of Secret Service men, a tall grey-haired man in a dark blue suit moved athletically down the steps, waving and smiling.

Anthony Jordan, the President of the United States.

Some people were getting to their feet.

Travis didn't know what do to. Stand at attention?

Without thinking, he began tapping his stick on the ice in salute. The rest of the Owls on the ice followed suit. The Owls on the bench stood and leaned over and rapped their sticks on the boards.

It was a wonderful moment. The cameras turned on the Owls and then on the Wall, all of whom began doing the same thing.

The President noticed and gave the Owls' bench the thumbs-up, which Mr. Dillinger returned. Muck didn't even notice. The puck was about to drop, and Muck was already lost in the play.

The President took his seat and the linesman moved back into position for the faceoff.

Travis looked up.

Chase Jordan was staring at him.

Chase winked.

Travis winked back.

The puck dropped.


"*H-h-h-helpppp!*" Nish called.

He could hear it well enough himself. But was the sound getting out?

He had chewed through and spat out enough of the foul-tasting tape to be able to call out. But any noise he made seemed to bounce right back at him.

*Was there any air getting in?* he suddenly wondered.

*What if he died in here?*

## 25

SAM DID HER BEST TO WORK THE PUCK OUT. SHE rapped it off the boards, stepped around the first forechecker, and moved as quickly as she could up towards the blueline before flipping the puck ahead to Sarah.

Sarah spun just as she gathered in the pass, her sudden movement to the side throwing off her check. She had enough space to move and dug in hard, moving up over centre, stickhandling and looking for a play.

Dmitri broke hard, cutting from the boards towards the centre of the Wall's blueline, and Sarah hit him with a perfect pass. Travis knew the play. If Dmitri was coming his way, he should go Dmitri's way. The criss-cross, a play to throw off the other team if they were trying to cover each player.

Dmitri carried the puck in, and both Wall defence, momentarily confused, moved to check him at the same time.

Dmitri saw them coming and dropped the puck. But he kept going, "accidentally" ploughing into the two defence. One went down with Dmitri, the other lost his stick.

Travis was in free, with nothing between him and the Washington goal but a stickless defenceman.

The defender lunged and fell, hoping to gather the puck into his body. Travis tucked the puck and stepped around the spinning defenceman.

*Completely free!*

He looked up. The Wall goalie was skittering out to cut off the angle. Travis knew exactly what he would do: fake the slapper, maybe draw the goalie out even more, then hold and cut for an angle shot, hoping the goalie wouldn't be able to recover and get back in time.

He raised his stick to fake the slapper.

The goalie went for it, driving hard towards Travis and going down to cut off the angles.

Travis held and swept around the goalie.

*Empty net!*

He had the tying goal. He aimed dead centre.

And suddenly his feet went out from under him.

"H–H–H–ELLLP!!!"

Nish could really yell now. He had chewed off and spat away most of the duct tape. He was yelling and screaming.

"H–H–HELP! . . . SAVE MEEEEE! . . . HHHELLLP MMMEEEEEE!!!!"

But nothing.

Nothing save his own desperate voice bouncing back at him.

He began to cry.

"PENALTY SHOT!"

Travis, still down on the ice, could hardly believe it. He had turned enough to see who had tripped him, and he had heard the referee's whistle. But he hadn't expected this. It was a penalty shot! His second of the tournament! And the player who had tripped him was *Chase Jordan!*

Sarah was tapping his pads as he got to his skates.

"It's up to you, Trav," she said. "We need you here."

The Owls needed the goal to tie. There were only forty-five seconds left on the clock. It was up to him.

Muck called them over to the bench. The other Owls would all have to be on the bench for the shot. Only Travis and the Wall goaltender would be on the ice.

The camera crews were all down at ice level now. They were acting like they were in charge, ignoring the referee and jumping over onto the ice to get the best shots. One crew was over at the Wall bench, the camera in the face of Chase Jordan, who was trying to ignore them.

Travis wished they would all go away. Why him? Why couldn't it be Sarah or Dmitri taking the shot? Or Nish? No one would enjoy all the attention more than Nish.

Everyone was on their feet, even the President.

Travis looked up, trying to clear his mind.

All he could focus on was Earplug, chewing his gum so fast it was a wonder smoke wasn't coming out his mouth.

"Lindsay," Muck said in a quiet voice. He was smiling. "Just remember to shoot this time, okay?"

The linesman placed the puck at centre ice, and the referee blew his whistle, the signal for Travis to start skating.

It all felt so dreadfully familiar: too much snow on the ice, a forty-pound puck, legs like wet spaghetti, arms of lead, brain of marshmallow.

Travis picked up the puck and bore down.

Muck had said it all: *just shoot the puck.*

Travis felt instantly better. His speed picked up. The puck lightened on his stick.

He reviewed what had happened just before the foul. The goalie had fallen for his fake slap-shot and Travis had tried to go around him. He'd be expecting Travis to try the same thing.

Travis pushed the puck over the blueline. High in the slot, he went into the same slapper motion.

This time the goalie stayed back, sure Travis would try to pull him out and get the angle on him.

It was one of Travis's better slappers. The heel of his stick caught the puck flush, and he was certain he could feel the puck roll along the length of his blade and spring off the slight curve at the end. The puck rose about a foot off the ground and smashed – *hard* – into the pads of the goalie.

"*No!*" Travis shouted to himself, spinning away and raising his eyes to the rafters.

Failed, again.

But then he saw the cheers go up from the Owls' bench.

Sarah threw her stick in the air.

Sam leapt up, screaming.

Fahd pumped his fists.

Travis turned back.

The puck had trickled through the goalie's pads! Tie game, 5–5.

They played out the final few seconds and the horn blew. The Presidential party was already headed for the Zamboni chute. But the championship game was tied. There would have to be sudden-death overtime.

The referee blew his whistle, consulted with the linesmen and then the off-ice officials.

He went over to both benches. "I'm ordering a flood," he told Muck. "There's too much snow on the ice to play."

"Good," Muck said. The Wall coach agreed.

All the players leapt over the boards onto their benches to wait out the quick flood.

"WHAT THE HELL DO YOU THINK YOU'RE DOING?" It was Earplug. He was screaming, hammering on the glass behind the off-ice officials' bench. He looked like he was about to burst.

"We can't play on this," the referee calmly explained. "I've ordered a fresh flood."

"YOU CAN'T DO THAT!" Earplug roared. "THIS IS THE PRESIDENT OF THE UNITED STATES. HE HAS A STRICT SCHEDULE TO STICK TO!"

"It's *my* call," the referee said, clearly fed up. "It's for safety reasons. These are peewee hockey players, not soldiers."

"I'M ORDERING YOU RIGHT NOW TO PROCEED WITH THE GAME INSTANTLY!" Earplug screamed.

The referee shook his head. "You're in charge of nothing here, pal, so relax. Five minutes, that's all it takes."

Earplug slammed his fist so hard against the glass Travis thought it would shatter. He stomped away towards the Presidential party. The President himself was busy talking to people in the crowd and shaking hands. He didn't seem in the slightest concerned about a five-minute delay for a flood. If anything, he was welcoming the opportunity to do a little campaigning.

Earplug needs a vacation, Travis thought to himself.

## 26

NISH WAS ALREADY SCREAMING WHEN HE HEARD the roar.

He was screaming and crying, convinced he was going to smother in this airtight box, when, suddenly, there was a slight whining noise, then the sound of something catching, coughing, then an enormous roar.

Mr. Dillinger took the opportunity to race back to the dressing room. He had five minutes to check the room and around most of the rest of the lower arena for Nish.

Mr. Dillinger was getting worried. He was responsible for the kids off the ice. He prided himself on taking great care of the team, without being *too* protective. But right now he felt terrible. *He had lost Nish.*

He checked the Screech Owls' dressing room, and the equipment rooms, and even the other dressing rooms. He checked the washrooms and corridors. He asked Secret Service guards at two rear doors and at the Zamboni main doors if they'd seen a chubby little kid in full hockey uniform, but no one had seen him.

*That smell. What was that smell?*

Nish knew it from somewhere. It was like . . . like . . . like *rotten eggs*! Yes, that was it. Rotten eggs.

Had he smelled it in science class? Fahd's old egg salad sandwiches he kept forgetting in his locker?

He felt a motion. Whatever he was in seemed to jump and chug and roll. And then the roar again – a huge roar.

His nose filled once more with a fresh burst of the rotten-egg smell.

But now he knew what it was.

Not rotten eggs, but *propane fuel*!

He felt his little prison cell moving now, smooth and fast. He heard all kinds of new sounds: valves turning, water running, something twisting, something grinding.

He felt something being sprayed onto him. Something cold, very cold.

Something like ground-up ice, or *snow*!

He knew now. He knew exactly where he was.

*Inside the Zamboni!*

## 27

MUCK LOOKED UP AS MR. DILLINGER CLIMBED back onto the bench. Mr. Dillinger looked crushed. He shook his head at Muck, but it was already obvious. Everything Mr. Dillinger had to say was on his face. No Nish.

"We could use that crazy idiot right about now," said Sam.

Travis saw that Sam was beyond worry. She was afraid for Nish. He realized how much Sam liked Nish, even if she never let on for a moment. The same for Sarah, who was biting her lip and staring out at the Zamboni as if it, somehow, held the answer.

"HHHHELLLPPPPPP!"

"I'M HERE – INSIDE THE ZAMBONI!"

The louder Nish screamed, the more his voice seemed to be lost in the roar of the machine.

The smell of the propane was much stronger now. He was breathing in fumes. His head was throbbing. His eyes stung. He was gagging. The snow was churning in on him. He didn't know how much longer he could hold out.

The thought came to him in a flash. He'd use his skates! His hands were tied in duct tape, but whoever had tossed him in here had done nothing to his legs. He could bang his skate blades against the metal sides of the Zamboni.

He kicked hard.

*Bang! Bang! . . . Bang! Bang! Bang! . . . Bang! Bang!*

"*Do you hear that?*" Sarah turned her head.

"Hear what?"

"Something's banging in the Zamboni!"

Travis listened hard. "Yeah," he said, "I do hear something."

"So do I," said Sam.

"Wait'll it comes around again," said Sarah.

The Zamboni made a wide turn, the ice glistening wet behind it, and headed back up-ice, drawing closer to the Screech Owls' bench.

At first the sound was faint. But then, as the big ice-surfacing machine drew alongside the bench, the sound grew considerably louder.

*Bang! Bang! . . . Bang! Bang! Bang! . . . Bang! Bang!*

That familiar rhythm . . . *It was Nish!*

Sarah stood up, screaming at the Zamboni driver. "*Stop!* STOPPPPP!"

Sam was already over the boards.

"STOPPPPP!"

## 28

"ANOTHER FEW CIRCLES AND WE MIGHT HAVE lost him."

Nish was under the care of the President's own personal doctor. He had come running down onto the ice immediately after Travis and Sam and Sarah had forced the Zamboni driver to stop.

The driver had been furious. No one was to come onto the ice when the machine was re-surfacing, he yelled at them. It was dangerous.

And then he, too, had heard the banging.

He had reached up and pulled a lever. There was the sound of valves moving and gears shift-ing, and slowly, like some yawning prehistoric monster, the Zamboni had opened up. Inside, half covered in snow and ice chips, was Nish, still screaming and pounding his skates against the insides of the huge machine.

"Either the snow would have smothered him," the doctor was saying, "or the fumes would have killed him."

"He's used to fumes," said Sam. The doctor looked at her, but he didn't get it.

The Screech Owls were all in the dressing room, waiting. Nish was in the corner, his skates kicked off and his face beaming red, but he hardly looked ill. He had two Cokes going at once and seemed, once again, delighted with all the attention.

But the big news story was unfolding outside the dressing room. The television crews that had come to get some footage of the President at a hockey game were now going live with a much different story.

*A threat on the life of the President!*

Travis was stunned by how quickly the Secret Service had moved. The building had been cleared at once. Both teams dispatched to their dressing rooms with guards on the doors. A complete investigation had taken place in less than an hour.

Two older men, one Secret Service, the other a presidential aide, had come around to the Owls' dressing room to explain.

Nish had come across an act of sabotage. The plan had been to assassinate the President as he was stationed in the Zamboni chute waiting to present the championship trophy – presumably to his son, Chase.

High-tech plastic explosives had been smuggled in past security and wired to explode when a signal was transmitted from a hand-held device by the assassin, who was also in the building.

The security camera in the Zamboni area had been tampered with so that it failed to cover that small space in the corner where the explosive had been planted.

The worst part, the Secret Service man said, was that the suspect in custody was "one of our own."

But Travis already knew that. He knew now why that little block of wood had been placed next to the security camera in the Zamboni chute.

He knew now why a certain person had seemed so nervous.

He knew now why there had been such yelling and screaming about a silly flood.

Only one person knew that Nish had been bundled into the Zamboni, and that once the Zamboni was back on the ice it was only a matter of time before Nish would be discovered, alive or dead, and the opportunity to kill the President would be lost.

The assassin was Earplug.

"Why would he?" Fahd asked the men.

The answers were shrugs. "We have no idea," the Secret Service man said. "We hope to find out. He might well have been acting alone. Obviously, he had become a very sick person without us noticing. And it's our job to notice."

There was a knock at the door and a man walked in, another of the President's aides. He smiled at the Screech Owls and nodded appreciatively to Nish, who had helped avert a terrible disaster. Had they not discovered him and then checked the chute, they would never have found the explosives.

"President Jordan has asked that the game continue," the man said. "The ice is ready."

The Owls cheered.

Nish reached down and picked up his skates. He handed them to Mr. Dillinger.

"Can I get a quick sharp," he said. "I think I took a bit of the edge off them."

Mr. Dillinger took the skates, his eyes wide in shock. Nish was going to play? Not even an hour ago he had been facing death!

Mr. Dillinger looked questioningly at the doctor, who smiled back.

"Probably the best thing for him," he said.

"Can I play?" Nish said to Muck.

Muck seemed to think about it awhile. Then he nodded. "You were on the game score sheet. Nothing says you have to see ice before overtime, I guess."

"LET'S GO!" shouted Sam, who slammed her stick into Nish's pads as she jumped up.

## 29

**THE ICE WAS PERFECT.**

Travis took a few easy loops around the rink before the officials came out to start the overtime. He was glad to get back to the game. He tried not to think about what had almost happened. Earplug, for whatever reason, had wanted to kill his President. Maybe he was a double agent, or maybe simply insane. He hadn't even given a thought to all the other deaths and injuries the explosion might have caused. Earplug could have been killed himself.

Nish made it out just before the game got underway again. He seemed a bit wobbly as he checked out Mr. Dillinger's sharp on his skates, but he also seemed keen to play.

The overtime started and the Owls got an early chance. Sarah hit Travis with a quick pass and he managed to squeeze between the boards and the Wall defenceman, popping free with the puck along the left side and no one between him and the goalie.

He wished he'd shot. Muck always said, "You can't go wrong with a shot." But he'd seen Dmitri swooping in from the far side and tried to hit him with a pass, only to have the other Wall defender dive onto his stomach and reach his stick out to jab the puck away.

The Owls had other chances. Little Simon broke in but hit the post. Fahd almost scored from the point, but the Wall goaltender stacked his pads and just got enough of the puck to deflect it clear. Sam had a clear shot and put it right into the goalie's chest.

Nish began slowly, but he was regaining his form. Once, he carried end to end, only to have a good slapper go off the outside of the far post.

The Washington Wall had chances too, but Jeremy was spectacular in net.

Up and down the game went. Shift after shift, Travis tried to create something, but nothing was happening for his line. Sarah couldn't break through. Dmitri couldn't use his speed to get clear. The line they were on against couldn't get anything going, either. It was that tight a match.

Travis was on the bench when Fahd pinched up and lost the puck. A Wall winger plucked it off the boards and sent a high sailing pass out over centre. He hadn't even meant it as a pass, just a clearing shot, but Chase Jordan had anticipated perfectly.

Chase caught up to the puck around centre. Wilson was chasing, but he lacked the speed to make up the gap. Chase moved in fast on Jeremy, who came out to cut out the angle. He shot hard. Jeremy caught it with his blocker – a fabulous save! – but the puck bounced right back into Chase Jordan's chest, fell to the ice, and Chase rapped it in on the rebound.

*The Wall were champions!*
*The President's son was the hero!*

Travis felt the sag on the Owls' bench. It was as if the air had gone out of the entire team. He turned and looked at Muck, who was already walking up the bench lightly touching each and every Owl on the back of the neck – his little message that they'd done their best, that there was no shame in losing such a great game. And in fact Travis felt good for Chase Jordan. In a way, this was how it *had* to end after all that had happened.

It was Travis who began the salute. He stood up, leaned over with his stick, and began pounding the boards with it. Sam and Sarah joined in, and soon all the Owls on the bench were doing it. The six Owls on the ice, Jeremy included, began slamming their sticks on the ice.

The crowd took up the chant. They clapped in time with the pounding sticks.

Chase Jordan broke out of the backslapping scrum of Washington Wall players and circled towards the Screech Owls' bench, raising his own stick to return the Owls' salute.

The rest of the Wall followed suit.

The Zamboni chute was opening. Two men were wheeling out a table, and on the table was the championship trophy. Right behind came the President of the United States, his shoes sliding on the still-clean ice.

The teams lined up on their bluelines for the presentation. The TV cameras were all back on the ice to record it on video.

The President made a little speech, only parts of which Travis could catch in the echoey arena, and then Chase Jordan, his helmet and gloves off, skated over to accept the trophy from his father.

It was a wonderful moment. So close to being a disaster.

Travis felt a chill run up and down his spine. He didn't think he'd want to live life the way Chase Jordan and his father lived it. Better to be safe in Tamarack, with only practice and homework to worry about.

Chase handed the trophy to his assistant captain, who raised it high over his head and began a Stanley Cup parade around the rink, while the crowd cheered them.

Chase left the group and skated back to the Owls. He high-fived the Owls until he came to Nish. "My father wants to speak to you."

"You *told*!" Nish shrieked, his eyes widening.

Chase Jordan laughed. "No – don't be silly. He wants to say something to you."

With the cameras following, and the colour in Nish's face rising, Chase Jordan and Nish skated over to where the President stood, smiling.

Travis watched the President lean over, say something to Nish as they shook hands, and then, with his other hand, give him something in a small blue box. Nish looked at it as they continued talking. Travis could swear Nish was glowing ever redder.

Nish skated back to the cheers of the crowd and the pounding sticks of the players. He was staring with an odd expression at the tiny blue box he held in his hands.

"*What is it?*" Fahd shouted.

"*What did he give you?*" Sam yelled down the line.

Nish held the box out and opened it for his teammates to see: tiny silver buttons with the Presidential seal on them.

"*Cufflinks!*" Andy shouted, laughing. "*You don't even own a suit!*"

Nish was now a deep, deep crimson. "That's what *I* said."

"Well," said Sarah, "what did he say back to you?"

Nish's face looked like it was about to burst.

"He said maybe I could wear them with my birthday suit."

**THE END**

THE NEXT BOOK IN THE SCREECH OWL SERIES

## The Secret of the Deep Woods

It is summer, and Rachel Highboy, Jesse's hockey-playing cousin from James Bay, has come to Tamarack to join the Screech Owls on a week-long canoe trip into the wilds of Algonquin Park.

At the same time, the rookie hero of this year's Stanley Cup final is in a light plane that goes missing somewhere in the area. It is eerily like the story of Bill Barilko, the legendary Toronto Maple Leafs defenceman who disappeared when his plane crashed deep in the Ontario bush in 1951, just four months after he scored the Stanley-Cup-winning goal!

When some of the team – including a terrified Nish – become separated from the others and find themselves lost in the deep woods, strange things begin to happen.

A wolf comes each night to stand by the campfire. A mysterious stranger pays a visit. And a shocking discovery has Rachel and the Screech Owls wondering if they'll make it out alive!

The Secret of the Deep Woods *will be published by McClelland & Stewart in the fall of 2002.*

## THE SCREECH OWLS SERIES

1. Mystery at Lake Placid

2. The Night They Stole the Stanley Cup

3. The Screech Owls' Northern Adventure

4. Murder at Hockey Camp

5. Kidnapped in Sweden

6. Terror in Florida

7. The Quebec City Crisis

8. The Screech Owls' Home Loss

9. Nightmare in Nagano

10. Danger in Dinosaur Valley

11. The Ghost of the Stanley Cup

12. The West Coast Murders

13. Sudden Death in New York City

14. Horror on River Road

15. Death Down Under

16. Power Play in Washington

17. The Secret of the Deep Woods (*fall 2002*)